WOMEN, SEATED

Women, Seated

ZHANG YUERAN

Translated by Jeremy Tiang

RIVERHEAD BOOKS
NEW YORK
2025

RIVERHEAD BOOKS
An imprint of Penguin Random House LLC
1745 Broadway, New York, NY 10019
penguinrandomhouse.com

Book design by Amanda Dewey

LIBRARY OF CONGRESS CONTROL NUMBER: 2024049338

ISBN 9780593851920 (hardcover)
ISBN 9780593851937 (ebook)
ISBN 9798217176748 (international edition)

First published in the People's Republic of China as 天鹅旅馆 by
Shanghai Sanlian Bookstore Co., Ltd, Shanghai, in 2024.
First United States edition published by Riverhead, 2025.
English language translation rights arranged with the
author through New River Literary Ltd.

Printed in the United States of America
1st Printing

The authorized representative in the EU for product safety
and compliance is Penguin Random House Ireland, Morrison
Chambers, 32 Nassau Street, Dublin D02 YH68, Ireland,
https://eu-contact.penguin.ie.

WOMEN, SEATED

1

Yu Ling got up especially early that April morning. Right away the faint scorch of sunlight on her blanket told her there was no hope of rain. Outside, the day was bright. She sat on the edge of her bed and looked out the second-story window. For half a month the magnolia tree had shed its blossoms, shrugging them off like an agitated woman. After the last few fell, it came to its senses overnight and was now a normal green tree once more. Yu Ling made the bed, placed her folded pajamas in the wardrobe, and went into the next room.

The boy was still asleep; she pulled back his covers. "Get up, quick. Spring outing today!"

The boy's eyes popped open. He tumbled out of bed and dashed into the bathroom to brush his teeth. From downstairs came Chopin's "Revolutionary Étude" on the record player, her sir's favorite tune. Yu Ling waited by the bathroom door with a gray sweater.

The boy came out and shook his head. "I want the yellow

one with the cars." He tried to wriggle away, but Yu Ling held him fast.

"We're going climbing. That one gets dirty too easily."

His trousers were gray too, and his shoes were an old black pair that he was starting to outgrow. The boy grumbled that he already looked grubby, even though they hadn't gone climbing yet. Yu Ling ignored him.

"Want to bring a toy?" she asked.

"Teddy."

"The talking bear?" She shook her head. "Too noisy." Instead, a pale yellow elephant went into the rucksack. "You used to like this one, remember?"

The boy ran downstairs. On the dining table stood a row of Tupperware filled with pineapple and cantaloupe, hulled strawberries, and the boy's favorite, peaches. The fruit was merely dessert. For the main course there were meat and seafood kebabs. Yu Ling had promised the boy a proper barbecue. "Proper" meaning all the food would be on skewers. She'd spent the previous evening threading meat onto sticks, and now everything she looked at seemed to have a hole in it. Hui, the other nanny, came in from the garden with a watering can.

"My god, are you really taking so much stuff?"

"Are you coming with us, Auntie Hui?" said the boy.

"I should be so lucky."

The boy's father came downstairs in exercise clothes, probably on his way to the gym.

"Got the gas cylinder?"

"I'm bringing two spares," Yu Ling replied, her eyes unfocused as usual. Her sir never looked at her, to avoid the insult of her not meeting his gaze. Right now, he was staring at the carved rosewood chair they'd bought not long ago.

"Bring a portable stereo so Kuan Kuan can listen to music along the way." He had an inflated estimation of his son's musical talent and was always nagging him to practice. Just a couple of days ago, the boy refused to go to his piano lesson, so her sir kicked his Lego castle until it lay in pieces—the one the boy and his grandfather had spent a full day building when he last visited. The boy had sworn never to forgive his father for it, and now he refused to turn around even when he called him several times as they were setting off.

Yu Ling loaded the Tupperware into the white duffel bag and hefted it onto the trolley, balancing a folding grill atop it. One hand steered the trolley, the other held the boy's hand.

"Zip up your coat," she said to the boy. "We'll be walking quite a ways."

The boy made a grab for the cart, and glass clink-clanked in the bag. On the grass verge, sprinklers sprayed an umbrella of mist and the sun beamed a miniature rainbow onto it. The boy stopped and counted on his fingers.

"Why only four colors? When can I see a complete rainbow?"

"I don't know, maybe the next time it rains."

"When will that be?"

"We can't have a spring outing in the rain. Which do you want, outing or rainbow?"

The boy stuck out his tongue and ran ahead, dragging the trolley after him. They passed a bed of crimson tulips as they walked around the man-made lake to the main entrance. From the shore, a maintenance worker was trying to scoop a dead fish from the water, using a long-handled net meant for leaves. Seeing them approach, he immediately stopped what he was doing and nodded at them. Outside the main gate, Yu Ling led the boy down the street. At the next turning, a battered white van was parked beneath a large tree, its paint mottled, one of its rear hubcaps bent out of shape. The family's driver, Dong, had been supposed to take them, but he was needed to pick up construction materials for the renovations on another house they owned. Yu Ling told him never mind, she knew someone from her hometown who could drive them.

The van door opened and the driver jumped out. The boy blinked at him.

"I thought you were Uncle Melon? You don't look like a melon."

The man grinned. "Wait till I shave my head, then you'll see how round it is."

The boy walked around the van, pausing behind it to study its rear. Yu Ling had to shout his name a few times before he came running back to the front. She opened the door and told him to climb in, then fastened his seat belt loosely across his chest. "I'll sit in front—Uncle Melon doesn't know the way."

Uncle Melon immediately protested, "I've been in Beijing more years than you!"

Yu Ling sat in the passenger seat. The man started the engine; the van swayed a few times, then wobbled into life. Excited to be in an unfamiliar vehicle with no child seat, the boy wriggled free from his seat belt, slid from one end to the other, and stood to reach for the roof until Yu Ling noticed and yelled at him to sit down.

The man steered with one hand, reaching for a cigarette with the other. It drooped from the corner of his mouth as he gestured for the lighter on the dashboard. Yu Ling flicked it, but the flame sputtered out.

"Silly." The man stuffed the cigarette between her lips.

Yu Ling turned to face the window. She didn't want the boy to see her with a cigarette. She lit it, only taking the quickest puff before passing it back. The man pulled a face in the rear-view mirror and waggled the cigarette.

"Want to try?"

"Are you crazy? He's only seven!" said Yu Ling.

"I was going to street fights with my brother when I was seven," said the man.

"I don't have a brother," said the boy solemnly.

The man burst into laughter. "So it's your parents' fault? Seems you're good at finding excuses."

2

The van turned off the busy road onto the highway where it could speed up, making the windows hum. Yu Ling took her phone from her fanny pack and glanced at it. As she put it back, her hand brushed against the mini stereo. She pulled it out: the silvery disc, full of little holes, looked like a beehive. When its surface caught the sunlight, it was as if honey was dripping out of it.

"What did you bring that for? There's a radio in the van," said the man.

"The sound quality is better. What music do you have on your phone?"

"You saying you can hear the difference? I only have xiang-sheng comedy on my phone."

"I want comedy!" The boy clapped his hands. "I've never heard comedy before."

"You've got to be kidding me," the man muttered. He

tapped his phone and a strange noise came from the speaker. Before the boy could make out the words, laughter overtook them. The boy laughed too and kept chuckling along with the recording. He pressed his face to the speaker as if to hear the laughter as soon as possible, the better to echo it.

Yu Ling turned to look at him. "Don't bite your nails." Her voice came out too thin for the boy to hear, but she didn't repeat herself. She rested her head on the back of her seat.

The man eyed her. "What's up?"

"Leave me alone." She shut her eyes.

She told herself she ought to nap for a while, there was still some time before they left the city. Yet she felt as if she couldn't shut her eyes tight enough to stop the sunlight from seeping into them. She clearly heard the man fiddling with the lighter and smelled his cigarette smoke. Then a window opened: a rush of wind, the hair at her temples leaping like flames. Wind dying down, quickly rising again, clutching at her scalp, drumming her forehead. She was certain she'd forgotten something. The notion had caught hold of her as soon as she left the house and was growing stronger by the minute. She tried hard to remember, but her head was like a pot full of porridge—stirring it just made the mess more gluey. The next time she opened her eyes, they were in the countryside, a borderless expanse of fields full of little golden-yellow flowers. Rapeseed. She had to think for a moment to retrieve the name. She'd been in the city too long, and flowers were now expensive items with a lifespan of a week. Who was the first person to cut flowers and sell them? What a mind.

It was Sunday, she now remembered, which meant a delivery from the flower market. The short florist usually parked his van at the villa gate and opened the rear compartment for Yu Ling to choose. Wild lilies, peonies, buttercups. Yu Ling would clutch her selection to her chest, the petals still dewy—though she knew very well this wasn't dew, but rather the man had misted them an hour ago. Still, an ordinary Sunday, transformed by fresh blossoms.

She'd miss the flowers today. Hui would take her place at the gate. It had been Hui's job in the first place, but her ma'am complained that Hui's taste was awful. Not everyone could be like Yu Ling, knowing the name of every variety, with her own system of flower arranging. Her ma'am had studied ikebana for a while but lacked patience, and was always thrusting her half-finished arrangements at Yu Ling. "You really have a talent for this. I want to excavate your potential," she insisted.

Her ma'am was due back that afternoon, or maybe evening. She frequently missed her flights and had to reschedule, but was never apologetic—she believed that punctuality was humiliating for an artist. This trip to Hong Kong had been a last-minute decision. Lacking inspiration, she'd gone in search of it at an auction. Sure enough, she'd proclaimed on the phone the day before that she'd nabbed a folding screen from India.

"Excellent," said her husband as always. "We'll celebrate when you're home."

"I'll be back tomorrow."

Yu Ling and Kuan Kuan had exchanged glances. The boy understood that once his mother was home, the spring outing would be iced. She would say there's nothing educational about a picnic, better to attend an art exhibition or concert.

"If you want to go," said Yu Ling to the moody boy, "we'll have to do it tomorrow morning before your ma gets back." The boy jumped to his feet with a whoop and flung his arms around her neck.

3

The boy sat with his cheek pressed against the window, motionless as a lizard. The comedy routine had lulled him into drowsiness.

The man turned on the radio. "Why can't we just listen to music on this?"

No sooner had he spoken when a buzzing came from the speakers, and a burst of singing quickly decreased in volume like a balloon drifting away into the sky. After a moment, the static got quieter, and the music bounced back into place. The singer got out two lines in his bass voice before the noise came back, more vigorous than ever. Yu Ling clapped her hands over her ears and urged the man to switch it off. He stubbornly turned the dial until he managed to find a station with clear reception: the news. The National Health Commission would now include occupational diseases under the provision of Basic Public Health. Construction would soon begin on yet another high-speed train line. The newsreader's voice was clear as a bell, and for that alone they were grateful. It made everything she said sound like good news.

Perking up, the boy lowered the window and poked his head out.

"Get back in here!" Yu Ling yelled.

He responded by sticking out his entire torso and screaming into the wind.

Yu Ling swung around and asked the man to pull over.

"Calm down," said the man. "I'm keeping a lookout, no one's passing us."

"I don't care!"

The man glared at Yu Ling. "Stop overreacting. You need to keep ahold of yourself."

A huge truck appeared in front of them. The boy came back inside and studied it with interest. He pointed at the metal cage on the flatbed. "What's in there?"

Yu Ling ignored him, and the boy asked again. The man replied, "Maybe chickens."

"Where are they going?"

"To market," said the man. "Waiting to be slaughtered."

The boy fell silent. A short while later, he reached out to tap the man on the shoulder and asked him to stop. The man ignored him and started overtaking the truck. As they passed it, the boy stuck his head out and shouted at the truck driver, "Hey—hey! Stop!"

The driver slammed on the brakes. Right away the boy reached for the door handle, and Yu Ling screamed. The van pulled into the emergency lane and came to a standstill.

The man roared at the boy, "What do you think you're doing?"

Yu Ling said she'd go out with the boy if he promised not to run around on the highway. They found the truck driver crouched on the ground, inspecting his rear tires.

"Uncle, what do you have on the back of your truck?"

The driver scowled at him. "I thought you were telling me I had a flat."

The boy ran over to the flatbed and stood on tiptoe, trying to see. "Can I have a look?"

Yu Ling said to the driver, "Sir, do me a favor?" She beckoned the man over, took the pack from his hand, and offered the driver a cigarette. He tucked it behind his ear and lowered the tailgate. The man gave the boy a leg up so he could crawl onto the flatbed. The boy squatted to study the cage, which was full of white geese, so tightly squashed together they looked like a single feathery clump with long necks protruding through the bars.

"Swans!" he cried, delighted. "Ma and Ba took me on vacation last year, and I saw some on a lake."

Yu Ling didn't correct him—that would lead to questions about the exact difference between geese and swans, which she wasn't confident she could answer. She'd only seen swans on TV, gliding serenely across still waters as if they had no legs.

"Are you done?" she asked the boy.

"Can we bring them with us?"

Yu Ling made her face go stern. "If we buy the swans, there'll be no spring outing. You choose."

The boy plopped himself down on the flatbed. "No spring outing, then."

"Fine. We'll go home right now."

Yu Ling stomped back toward the van, but the man caught hold of her. "What are you playing at?"

"I want to go back. Today's not suitable for a spring outing."

"What are you talking about?" The man took another couple of fierce drags from his cigarette and tossed the butt away. He called to the driver, "How much?"

"Five hundred each."

The man's eyes widened. "That's daylight robbery!" Nonetheless, he pulled out his phone and transferred the money to the driver.

"You can only pick one," he told the boy.

"What will happen to the rest of the swans?"

"They'll go where they're supposed to go. Now hurry up and choose, we need to get going."

The boy pouted and looked at Yu Ling. The man looked at her too. After a pause, she told the boy, "We don't have much money. You can have one swan or no swans, you decide."

He reluctantly agreed, then immediately got caught up in the problem of which one to choose. All the geese were asleep, apart from one in the farthest corner of the cage, whose gleaming black eyes were wide open. "That one," he said. When the driver opened the cage they all blinked awake, retreating in a frenzy. The driver went to grab one at random, but the boy insisted he wanted the one that had caught his eye. He scanned the cage, left to right, right to left. The driver straightened up impatiently and stood with his hands on his hips.

"That one!" The boy pointed at a goose and spread his arms wide, ready to embrace it. The driver's large hand came down on its belly, causing it to let out a desolate cry. The boy flung his arms over his own head and crouched down. He stayed there until the driver had tied the goose's legs and handed it over.

"Won't it fly away?" said the boy.

"If it knew how to do that, it wouldn't be where it is now," said the man. "I've told Auntie Yu we'll still go on the spring outing, but you can't cause any more trouble. Got it?"

"But it *can* fly. I've seen swans fly."

The goose was stowed in the back seat. Yu Ling placed the boy's rucksack between them and warned him not to reach across. "Be careful or you'll get bitten."

The van started moving, windows rattling. The newsreader resumed her broadcast. The boy slid a hand beneath the rucksack, like a soldier lying an ambush, moving forward a little whenever he got the chance, then stopping to assess the situation.

Yu Ling's phone rang. She pulled it from her tote bag and saw it was her sir. When she answered, he said something urgent had come up and she should bring Kuan Kuan home immediately. He hung up before she could say anything.

"What's going on?" asked the man.

The boy stood up on the back seat and yelled, "I'm not going back!"

"Sit!" shouted Yu Ling.

He sat, and calmed down when he saw that the van was still going full speed ahead. His hand went right past the rucksack and arrived at the goose's feet.

On the radio, the newsreader said a cold front was moving south, and temperatures would drop the next day. Then it was noon, and she began the news bulletin. They turned off the highway and into a gas station.

Yu Ling pulled open the rear door and said to the boy, "Go ahead and use the bathroom."

He glanced at the goose.

"I'll watch it," said Yu Ling. "It's not going anywhere."

The boy jumped out and headed to the bathroom, turning every few steps as if something was drawing him back.

"I know what makes this van different!" he announced triumphantly to the man. "It doesn't have license plates."

The man walked past him, blank faced. Yu Ling stood by the van, her head thrown back as she guzzled some water. The man came over to her.

"Did you turn off your phone?" he said. She nodded. "You'll have to get rid of the SIM card too."

"When we're past the tollbooth."

"Still haven't made up your mind?"

"Could you stop speaking to me? I need a bit of quiet."

4

The van went up the ramp to the highway, which ascended until it was level with the tops of the poplar trees. Their crowns swayed in the breeze, branches parting and coming together again. The sky was gray, the sun behind a layer of fog.

The boy leaned forward, observing the two adults in front. A few minutes ago, he'd informed them he was hungry, but hadn't received a response. The van was very quiet. Even the rattling of the window was no longer noise, but part of the silence. The radio was still on, but no one was listening. Then the music abruptly fell away and the newsreader returned.

"According to the Central Disciplinary Commission, former Yunnan Province Party Secretary Qin Xinwei is under investigation for a serious breach of the law, and is currently assisting the commission with their inquiries. Qin was born in January 1954 in Luoyang, Henan Province, and entered the workforce in February 1971. A Party member, he has a doctorate in economics . . ."

"Grandpa!" hollered the boy. "Grandpa's name is Qin Xinwei!"

"Quiet!" said Yu Ling. She turned the volume up.

"This is the first investigation of a province-level official this year."

"What's an investigation?" asked the boy. No one answered.

The man smacked the driving wheel with both palms and swiftly pulled over to the side of the road. The goose tumbled to the ground and flapped its wings in a panic. The boy went to hug it, only to get nipped by its beak.

The boy thrust his injured hand in his pocket and asked again, "What's an investigation?"

After a moment, Yu Ling turned around. "Your grandpa's gone to have a meeting." Inspired by the truck driver, she said, "I think there's something wrong with our tires. I'll go have a look."

The man got out too. They met round the back of the van.

"What rotten luck," said the man. "This is your fault. We'd have been fine if we'd done this sooner."

Trying to sound unworried, Yu Ling said, "I told you, I had a sense today wasn't the right time."

"There'll never be a right time! Don't you understand? That family is finished."

"Maybe the investigation won't turn up anything? For all we know, he'll be able to go home once they've looked into it."

"Go home? Don't you ever watch the news? He'll spend the rest of his life in jail. His daughter and her husband will get sucked into it too. Qin Wen's an only child, right?"

This sounded a bit over the top to Yu Ling. How serious

could Qin Xinwei's crimes be? He hadn't actually killed anyone, right?

The boy jumped out and crouched to look at the tires. When
he was done inspecting the front ones, he came round to the
back.

The man glared at him as he walked past. "I'm going to
phone his ba now."

"Not today, the family's been through enough."

"Their money belongs to the people, and we're the people,
so what does it matter if we take a little of it?"

"What does it matter?" the boy parroted, coming to a halt.
He enjoyed picking up scraps of language from adults.

Yu Ling dragged him back into the van, shoving the goose
to one side so she could sit in the back seat too. Through the
window, she watched the man. Stubby neck, broad shoulders,
burly chest. He walked over to a tree and stood with one hand
on its trunk, his phone in the other. The sun glinted off its silvery plastic case.

He returned to the van and said he'd phoned Kuan Kuan's
ba, but hadn't been able to get through. He told Yu Ling to try.
If he answered, she'd say there'd been an accident and they'd be
late getting home. Yu Ling went back to the passenger seat, re-
inserted the SIM card into her phone, and tried calling. A flat
voice said the call couldn't be connected.

"Are you calling my ba?" said the boy.

"Try his ma," murmured the man.

Yu Ling did as he asked, and got a female voice: "The phone
you are trying to reach has been switched off." She put down
her phone.

No sound but the radio, the same newsreader with the weather forecast.

"I don't want to go home!" yelled the boy. Yu Ling ignored him. She called Dong, the chauffeur, but his phone was off too. As a last resort, she tried Hui. It rang, but no one answered.

"This is bad." The man leaned back in his seat, kneading an empty cigarette packet. He chuckled. "In a way, I saved you. They'd have taken you away too."

"Who wants to take Auntie Yu away?" asked the boy.

The van started again and kept moving forward, to the boy's relief. He quietly took the hand from his pocket, inspected the red beak mark, and whispered to the goose, "I don't blame you, I know you're in a bad mood."

The van turned off the highway, and the road ahead became a dirt track, throwing up clouds of dust. The track was bumpy, causing the van to sway violently. Startled, the goose flapped and fidgeted, ending up on the floor again. When the boy made a move toward it, its head twisted and it looked ready to peck at him. The boy held up his hands in surrender and pulled back.

"Are we lost?" he asked, to silence.

Yu Ling kept trying the same numbers until the news came on again.

"According to the Central Disciplinary Commission, former Yunnan Province Party Secretary Qin Xinwei is under investigation for a serious breach of the law, and is currently assisting the commission with their inquiries. Qin was born in January 1954 . . ."

Yu Ling glanced at the man. "That's just the same as before, nothing new."

"Obviously. Did you think it's a radio serial? We won't find out the ending yet."

They finally reached the end of the dirt track and turned onto a narrow paved road.

"Waterfall! Waterfall!" yelped the boy. Yu Ling looked out the window. To their right was a reservoir with its sluice gates open, allowing water to flow half a meter to a lower pool.

The man wanted to park, but Yu Ling said they were too close to the water, and there was no embankment. She made him go a little farther, round the bend to the far side of the reservoir. There was a grove of trees here, and a low hill behind them blanketed with completely unremarkable vegetation.

The man pulled the hand brake. Yu Ling got out and opened the rear door. "You can play here," she said to the boy, "but make sure I can see you. Understand?"

She returned to the passenger seat, where the man began shouting, "Didn't I tell you, these government officials get arrested all the time?"

"Everyone's disappeared," said Yu Ling, lost in a sort of excitement.

"Are you happy about this? I knew you were a weirdo."

The phone rang. With a flicker of disappointment, Yu Ling saw Hui's name on the screen.

"Two men came and took Kuan Kuan's ba away," said Hui. "He wanted you to call the boy's grandmother. The number's in a brown notebook."

"What about his ma?"

"She's not back yet. Not long after you left, Kuan Kuan's ba came back from the gym and made a long phone call in the home office. When he was done, he told me to pack a bag for Kuan Kuan. I asked where they were going, but he wouldn't tell me. By the time I'd finished, the men had arrived. They were very polite. Wanted to know who normally lived here." Hui paused. "Will you be back soon?"

Yu Ling said they were still some distance away, and Hui said, "Okay, I should go. You also get your wages at the end of the month, don't you? They owe us, you know."

"Just take whatever you want, you don't need to find excuses," said Yu Ling. "Not like it's ever stopped you before."

Hui laughed. "Don't worry about me, you should be thinking about your own future. The agency knows about your background now—you won't find it so easy to find another job." She hung up. Yu Ling snapped her phone off and flung it into her bag, as if it was in league with Hui.

"Any energy you have, you spend fighting with other women." The man tossed his cigarette butt out the window. "Listen, the boy's ma probably hasn't been arrested yet. We need to get hold of her and tell her we have the kid."

"The police haven't been able to track her down—you think you can?"

"Does she have any friends in Hong Kong? Think!"

Yu Ling looked out the window. The boy was crouched amid the long grass, examining something green and wriggling in his hands. Maybe a caterpillar?

"She has no friends." The words brought a spark of joy to Yu Ling's heart.

5

"'Just treat this as a spring outing, don't think about anything else.' Isn't that what you told me?" Yu Ling opened the rear doors of the van and lifted out the trolley of barbecue stuff. "I'm just doing like you said."

She dragged the grill over to the shade of a tree, set it up on a flat patch of ground, and went back for the gas canister. This wasn't difficult, she'd seen other people doing it. The man watched, hands on hips, then went off to one side to make another phone call. Yu Ling spread the blue-and-white-checkered blanket on the ground and began unpacking the canvas bags. It wasn't just cut fruit and meat skewers she'd prepared the night before; she'd brought enough to last them three days. According to the plan, they were supposed to drive to the Hebei border, where they could hide out on deserted Mount Cangyan for as long as negotiations took, which the man had promised would be no longer than three days. He'd also guaranteed the kid wouldn't know what was going on—they'd just say they'd gotten lost and their phones weren't working. When they got the ransom, they'd bring him back to Beijing, leave him at an amusement park on the outskirts of the city, and contact the parents once they were well out of the way. She'd chosen the amusement park: they'd been there before, and though it didn't have many paying customers these days, at least there'd be workers the boy could go to for help after he realized she'd "lost" him. Yes, she'd planned to say farewell to the boy in this place. But this was inevitable; she'd have had to have left sooner or later, and their separation would be permanent. She wasn't holding out hope that he'd track her down decades later, traveling all the way to her village to visit his former nanny.

The boy would think of this as a spring outing, albeit a longer than usual one, she'd told herself. Food and board games would while away the time. Perhaps the boy would have so much fun, he'd miss her. A shameful thought, wanting the boy to miss her. Mortified, she'd gone ahead and packed a feast: Australian Wagyu beef, Angus beef tongue, Mongolian lamb chops, French black cod, Hokkaido scallop sashimi, New Zealand black gold abalone, scarlet carabineros prawns, Alaskan snow crab legs, jamón ibérico, drunken crab, porcini.

All of these came from the icebox in the basement of the house, each item replenished whenever it was running low. As with their fresh flowers, the family had a dedicated food supplier, though these deliveries arrived not at regular intervals but as needed, more frequently when they'd been throwing parties. This supplier's most important task was seeking out rare seasonal ingredients: maitake, blue bolete mushrooms,

Japanese saury. Sometimes he'd bring wild mountain mush-rooms, and her sir would have a dinner party to show them off.

Yu Ling called Kuan Kuan's name a couple of times before the boy slowly walked over, hands cupped. She stopped brushing oil on the grill and looked at him. "What have you got there?"

"A grasshopper?" he said uncertainly. "Are grasshoppers wild animals?"

"Let it go. Aren't you hungry?"

"Are grasshoppers carnivores? Do they eat beef?"

"No."

"Then—"

Before he could finish his next question, Yu Ling inter-rupted. "Geese don't eat beef either, but maybe they eat grass-hoppers. Why don't you give it a try?" The boy pulled his hands back to his chest and shook his head.

"Keep holding on to it, then. You won't be able to eat any-thing."

The boy crouched down in a patch of grass, but his hands were still clasped when he stood up again. He went over to the man and cracked them open like a conjurer, giving him a glimpse of the grasshopper. The man was still fiddling with his phone and shooed him away. The boy kept hovering, so the man said he loved roasted grasshoppers, and made a grab for it. The boy scampered away.

When the beef skewers were done, Yu Ling moved them to a plate and laid the prawns and crab legs on the grill.

"Aren't you two eating?" she called, picking up a skewer. She'd seasoned them with only a few herbs, sea salt, and black pepper, to preserve as much beef flavor as possible. The meat was juicy, with a faint milky taste. She poured herself a cup of orange juice. The sun showed itself directly overhead, shining down staunchly on them, gleaming off the rim of her cup. Yu Ling thought about her ma'am, Qin Wen. She must have heard by now that her father and husband had been taken away. Her fair-weather friends would be keeping their distance. She's on the run, all alone, thought Yu Ling, and here I am lounging in the sun enjoying a beef skewer.

Kuan Kuan came over. He'd finally let the grasshopper go because his arms were tired. The man came too, frowning, clearly furious.

Yu Ling handed them a beef skewer each and returned to the grill.

"Is this from those fancy beer-drinking cows?" asked the man. "Isn't there any ketchup?"

The boy watched for a while, then ate like the man did: holding the bamboo skewer horizontally and running his fingers along it, pushing the meat and peppers toward his mouth. He hated peppers, though, and spat them out.

"From today, you need to stop being picky, understand?" she said from behind him.

"Why from today?" he asked. She didn't have an answer for that.

"Because from today, if you don't eat, you'll go hungry. Got it?" said the man.

Yu Ling crouched down with a napkin to wipe the grease from the boy's lips. "Because you're grown up."

"Today?" said the boy, startled, as if he'd missed something important.

"Yes, today."

"Why didn't you bring any booze?" groused the man.

"I didn't want you to drink too much and not be able to drive. You can't half-ass something this important. Isn't that what you taught me?"

"Fine." The man pointed at the snow crab legs on the grill. "Those things are so red, they've got to be dyed." He watched the boy eat one and, seeing how much he enjoyed it, said he wanted to try one too. He ended up finishing the rest.

"Anyone who eats this well all the time will pay for it eventually." There was a slick of oil on the man's nose. He rose unsteadily and went among the trees to pee. The boy followed him. As they returned, the man caught hold of him and asked whether his ma had any friends in Hong Kong. The boy said she had plenty, but could only think of two names: Limin and Grace.

"Uncle Melon, do people need to have friends?"

"Of course. You never know when you might need a helping hand." He glanced at Yu Ling.

She'd just finished grilling the cod and beef tongue and was moving them onto a plate to make room for the pitas. She also cut some slices of the walnut bread she'd baked the day before, and started toasting them.

"Do you prefer my cooking, or what you ate at that French family's house?" she asked Kuan Kuan.

"What French family? I don't remember."

"They had that huge golden retriever. There was a swing in the yard—you and their daughter were playing on it for ages."

"I didn't get to play, she made me push her the whole time," said the boy, recalling. "I hated her."

"I was asking about the food."

"Your cooking is better," said the boy. Yu Ling nodded and served him a mushroom.

"What's the use of cooking well? You're not going to see even a strand of hair from a Wagyu cow after this," said the man.

"Could you shut your mouth? I just want to have a nice meal."

"We need to talk turkey. Hey you, kid, go play over there."

The man asked Yu Ling whether Qin Wen had a friend named Limin. Limin was her aesthetician, said Yu Ling. Qin Wen thought the air-conditioning at the beauty parlor was too cold, so she summoned Limin to her home whenever she was in Hong Kong. "What about Grace?" said the man. Yu Ling couldn't remember anyone with that name.

"Doesn't matter. We have the kid. Qin Wen is sure to call you."

"How long are we holding him? Hu Yafei wanted me to contact Kuan Kuan's grandma to say Qin Wen can't come back for the time being."

"Let's bring the kid to the grandma and ask *her* for money, then."

Yu Ling protested that they needed to head back to the villa first, to find Hu Yafei's notebook, which held the grandmother's number. She lived in Nanning, Guangxi.

"Nanning?"

Hu Yafei was from Guangxi, said Yu Ling. His parents and siblings still lived there, but they didn't get on with Qin Wen, so they seldom saw each other. Nonetheless, the man insisted, the Hus weren't going to abandon the kid. He couldn't decide whether they ought to wait for Qin Wen to get in touch, or phone the grandmother right away. He paced beneath a tree, a cigarette in his mouth. Yu Ling stared at the leftover food: congealing beef, curling prawns. The spring outing was over. She let out a long sigh and began putting everything away. As she worked, she realized the boy was no longer in sight.

"Kuan Kuan!" she called. He answered from some distance away. She looked in that direction: just trees, no pond or anything dangerous like that. She dismantled the grill and pushed it on the trolley back to the van. One of the canvas bags was so full, the zipper snapped off when she tried to close it. Noticing a muddy white rug in the rear, she decided to wrap it around the gaping bag.

The rug was larger than she'd expected, and one corner was caught on something. She tugged at it till it came free, revealing the black nylon rucksack it had been covering, shoved deep in a corner. She opened it and found a hammer, a switchblade, and a coil of thick rope. Also, wrapped in a towel, a bottle of ether. She stuffed everything back into the rucksack and pushed it in the corner, where it clunked against something. She leaned in for a closer look and saw a shovel. A shiver went through her.

6

Hearing a flurry of footsteps, Yu Ling closed the trunk and swung around. Kuan Kuan came barreling toward her, throwing himself into her bosom.

"What's wrong?" she asked.

The boy looked up at her, his eyes full of tears. He took her hand and led her between the trees. It was quiet here and the ground was damp, the earth open like a scar. She hurried along, almost tripping over an exposed root. The trees got denser up ahead. She hadn't realized how far away the boy had roamed. He pressed her palm and stopped walking. She looked around but didn't see anything, until she followed Kuan Kuan's gaze to the white clump beneath the tree ahead of them. A dead cat. She wasn't sure at first, its posture was so odd: legs splayed, back arched, head drooping—an almost human pose. She went around and shrieked when she saw its face. Its eye sockets were empty, streaming with ants.

The summer after finishing middle school, she worked at

her uncle's chicken farm for a few months. They took good care of her and didn't make her slaughter a single fowl. Her only responsibility was cleaning the carcasses. She would pinch their necks, feeling the slippery skin beneath her fingers. A fear haunted her the whole time: that the chicken in her hands would suddenly blink open its eyes and stare at her. Her math was good enough that she knew there was such a thing as probability, and she believed if she handled enough chickens, this was bound to happen sooner or later. People are always encountering all sorts of strange events—who could guarantee this wouldn't be one of them? A not-quite-dead chicken reviving or, worse, a chicken returning from the dead. When she was a little older, she understood that this wasn't actually possible. Death is absolute. You can struggle and resist all you like from the side of the living, but once death arrives to carry you across the divide, you're never coming back.

She took Kuan Kuan's hand, but he pulled free. "We can't just leave it."

What should they do, then? Kuan Kuan thought for a moment. "We ought to bury it."

"Animals don't need to be buried."

"Why not? Let it sleep more comfortably." One day, while she was telling him a story, Kuan Kuan had asked why dead people needed to be buried, and this was the explanation Yu Ling had given. Sometimes you need a simple answer, as long as it's not too ridiculous. She'd thought she was being clever, but now she'd created more work for herself.

She headed back to the van, got the shovel from the rear, and returned to the tree. The man was still on the phone, ges-

turing energetically as if he was doing his best to explain something.

The boy watched solemnly as she dug into the earth. The
soil was compacted, and the scraping sound made her scalp
ache. She brought the shovel down even harder, forcing herself
to remember the noise, to remember why the shovel had shown
up in the van. Using both hands, she scooped up the cat and
placed it in the pit. It wasn't as stiff as she'd thought it would
be, and when she released it, it curled around itself. The boy
helped her fill in the grave, leaving a little mound.

Yu Ling tossed the shovel aside and took the boy's hand.
"Let's go."

They found the man rearranging things in the van. He
shoved the luggage farther in and shrugged at Yu Ling. She
bundled the boy into the rear seat, and instead of returning to
the front, pushed his backpack toward the goose so she could
get in next to him.

The man stuck his head in. "What are you doing?"

"I don't care what you've decided, we have to go back to
Golden Lake Villas right away. Or else—"

"Or else what?"

"You'd better do as I tell you," Yu Ling heard herself say.
She turned her gaze away from the man's face, looking straight
ahead. "Start the van."

The man stared at her for a moment, his hand on the door,
but eventually he retreated to the front and began driving.

The sky was getting darker. They sped along the highway. A
few flecks of moisture hit the windshield, as if it was about to
rain, but then they went away. The headlights came on, pitilessly

lighting up the vehicles ahead of them. The report of Qin Xin-wei's arrest came on the news again.

"I told the cat many things." The boy looked up at Yu Ling, eyes gleaming in the dark. "I said it doesn't matter that it has no friends, anyone can play by themselves." He reached out to pet the goose, making sure it was paying attention. The goose didn't move. It was probably asleep, and shortly before they reached the house, the boy nodded off too, his head resting against Yu Ling, his arm twining around hers. The van went over some roadworks, jolting them apart. He didn't open his eyes, but groped for her arm in the dark and hugged it.

7

Yu Ling went inside. The house looked the same, although the curtains hadn't been drawn, and the darkness beyond the large windows made the rooms look emptier than usual. On the dining room wall, facing the table, was a familiar oil painting of a young woman holding an infant, her arm pinning his to keep him from moving. Their heads touched as they looked ahead, eyes wide. The background was murky, as if they only had a single candle for illumination. Yu Ling walked over and turned on a lamp.

The boy's suitcase stood by the couch. On the coffee table was the mug her sir had used, and there was a half-smoked cigar in the ashtray. Her sir rarely smoked cigars in the morning.

Yu Ling told the boy his ba would be gone a few days on an urgent business trip. She was contemplating where to say he'd gone when the boy began jumping gleefully. "No more piano practice!"

The man brought in the goose and, when the boy begged

him to, untied it. The goose waggled its rump and ran around the living room. The man roamed about, picking up the bronze figurine from the credenza for a closer look, lounging in the black and white horsehide window seat. Then he came up behind Yu Ling and whispered, "Where's the safe?"

"I've never seen a safe here." Yu Ling went upstairs to Qin Wen's bedroom and pulled open the drawer of her vanity. The once-full jewelry box was nearly empty. In the dressing area, a whole shelf's worth of handbags had gone missing. She opened the closet and found quite a few gaps, particularly among the evening gowns and more expensive furs. Probably most of these would be sold off, but Yu Ling couldn't help imagining Hui in a fur coat, grinning to reveal her sharp little canines.

As Yu Ling emerged from the bedroom, she bumped into the man coming down the corridor, a gold fountain pen tucked behind his ear. He'd searched her sir's study and found nothing. His favorite watches, which Yu Ling remembered being in his desk drawer, were nowhere to be seen.

"Isn't there any other storage in this house?" asked the man.

"The wine cellar." She gave him a look. "You've been there."

"Who wants wine? Too heavy to transport. Where are the other valuables?"

"Every object in this house is valuable."

The man looked at the crystal chandelier above them, trying to work out if he could bring it down. Finally he dismissed it and went back downstairs.

Yu Ling tried to chase the goose into the garden so it wouldn't shit on the carpet. She was always vigilant around that Tibetan carpet, not letting the boy get cake frosting or cookie crumbs on it. That old thing was actually worth over two hundred grand. When the giver revealed the price, she'd been certain he was lying, but gradually realized it was true. No one would dare walk through the front door with a gift costing a mere few thousand.

The man had always liked the leather sofa set. Now he was relaxing in it, one arm across the back of the couch, legs crossed, looking every inch the sir. He seemed to sense something was missing, then his eyes landed on the cigar and he popped it into his mouth.

"The fat cigarette smells better than your thin cigarettes," said the boy, eyeing him. "But it still stinks."

"It's supposed to stink." The man flicked the lighter in the direction of the boy, who fled from its blue flame. Puffing at the cigar, the man turned on the TV and fiddled with the remote. There were countless channels, but most of them were in foreign languages. So many unsubtitled English films. He clicked on another signal source, and the room they were in showed up on the screen. The camera was pointing toward the back garden, taking in the rock formation and gazebo, the tearoom and her ma'am's art workshop. Kuan Kuan appeared with some other kids, feeding the fish in the pond. They were talking, but the audio had been removed, replaced by music. This wasn't just a recording, it had clearly been edited. Every color had been carefully enhanced, making the greens greener and the whites whiter, and the ladies' lipstick even more vibrant.

"That's my birthday!" said Kuan Kuan, going up to the screen. A clown in baggy trousers jumped out from behind a rock. "That's him!" yelled the boy. "He cheated when he did his magic tricks, I saw him tie a string around his coin." He asked the man to turn off the TV—he didn't want to watch the fraudster. When the man ignored him, the boy went round the back and pulled out a thumb drive, cutting out the signal and leaving a blank blue screen.

The man turned off the TV. He kept puffing at the cigar to keep it from going out, which looked exhausting. Then he hollered for Yu Ling to say he'd decided, they weren't going to wait for the boy's mother any longer, they should phone his grandmother right away. Yu Ling frowned and said nothing. She went over to the window and touched a button on the wall, which made the dark green curtains slowly slide shut.

"They won't let me off," said the man. In the tiny sliver of uncovered glass, Yu Ling could see his reflection. His mouth drooped and he was looking blankly at her.

She said he could make the call but shouldn't mention money for now. When the old woman arrived in Beijing to pick up the boy, they could ask her to help them out.

"We're taking care of the kid. She'll definitely reward us for that."

The man agreed. They went up to the study, and Yu Ling found her sir's brown notebook in the top drawer of his desk. The phone number was on the last page in big writing, every digit gone over multiple times, as if to make sure it wouldn't be misread. Or perhaps her sir had been annoyed while on the phone and traced over the writing for something to do. A raspy-voiced woman answered their call, and seemed unsurprised that Yu Ling was getting in touch. Kuan Kuan's grandmother had had a stroke, she said, and was in the hospital right now. The main point she wanted to convey was that she was very busy and didn't have time to talk. She said Yu Ling should call again the next day.

The man kicked the sofa viciously. "That's fucked up, that's really fucked up!"

Yu Ling rested her elbows on the table, fingers interlaced. "Let's walk away now."

"We are doing this—we agreed! How can you go back on your word just like that?"

"You almost got us into big trouble! If anything happened to the kid, how would we ever live with ourselves?" She looked down, softening her tone. "We'll find another way to sort out the money. If we have to, we can pay back a portion from my savings. Though you know I'm keeping that to build a house when we get married."

"Is that all you can think about, getting married?" The man huffily plonked himself on the sofa, then almost immediately jumped to his feet. "Wait, there's a security camera!" He pointed at a black sphere on the ceiling and stalked out of the room.

By the time Yu Ling came back downstairs, there was a green tent in the middle of the living room. The boy must have dug it up from the storeroom.

"This is Swan Home," proclaimed the boy. "Swan's sleeping here tonight, and so am I."

No one had informed the "swan" of this plan, though. It had found a pot of geraniums in a corner and was energetically rooting around in the soil with its beak. It was unmoved by the boy's invitation, until it saw the boy raising an arm as if to strike it, at which point it began running. The boy chased it around the room, herding it toward the tent. The goose kept passing the entrance flap, showing no interest in going in.

The man came down, having made another round of the upstairs. "There are hidden cameras all over this house. Someone might be watching us anytime." He took Yu Ling's phone from his pocket and put it on the table.

"What were you doing with my phone?"

"Don't use it for now. They might be listening in."

The man headed for the front door. Yu Ling made no move to walk him out.

He turned back to look at her. "I do want to make a go of it with you."

The boy ran over and tugged at the man's arm so he bent down, and whispered in his ear, "Uncle Melon, will you promise not to eat any more grasshoppers?"

"Stop calling me that. My name is Chen Donghu." The man shook off the boy's hand and left the house.

8

Yu Ling was back in her bed. A day ago, she'd thought that would be her final night in this room. Naturally she hadn't got much sleep, tossing and turning till almost dawn. When she finally dropped off, she dreamed of rain, torrents of water pouring from above—but when she opened her eyes it was dry, nothing in the sky but blazing sun. Then followed the excruciatingly long and nerve-racking day. They hadn't been able to carry out their plan, or rather they did what they'd intended to do, but it came to nothing in the end. Like writing words on water, like punching cotton wool. In the face of a greater power, their pitiful efforts were worthless. Before leaving the house yesterday morning, she'd told herself: *Once you take this step, there's no turning back*. Yet here she was, right back where she'd started, in the same old bed. And after a whole day driving back and forth, what could be more satisfying? She lay on her favorite lavender sheets, soft from repeated washing, faintly scented with sandalwood from the detergent. Her latex pillow was exactly the right height—she'd actually contemplated taking it with her. Although she was now exhausted, all of this was so comfortable she was reluctant to let go of the sensation by falling asleep.

She'd slept in this bed for four years now. First in the nursery, until Kuan Kuan turned four and her ma'am decided she wanted him to be more independent. After Yu Ling moved to this room, Kuan Kuan often came scampering in barefoot in the dead of night, groping his way to the bed and burrowing under the covers. He liked holding on to her ear as he dozed off, and when he couldn't sleep, he'd knead her earlobes with his plump little fingers. Just before dawn, Yu Ling would carry him back to his room and tell him this had to be their little secret. Sure, the boy would say delightedly, he liked when they had secrets. Then a few months later, he abruptly stopped visiting, but she still woke up promptly at three in the morning, listening for approaching footsteps. She knew she shouldn't feel hurt, it was just a job. She would leave this place sooner or later. Now she rolled over, and through the gloom she could make out a cute little sticker on the wall by the bed, a yellow creature that looked a bit like a chick. Kuan Kuan had pasted it there and told her, "Put your finger on its body and make a wish, it'll come true." Yu Ling couldn't say he was wrong because she'd never tried. Strangely, even though no one ever touched it, the Pokémon's long ears were becoming worn. According to Kuan Kuan, this meant its good fortune was transferring to her. Her lucky escape today was due to the Pokémon's missing millimeter of ear.

Everything felt normal. The thick darkness, the scent of the room, the ticking of the alarm clock on the bedside table. And yet, nothing seemed right when Yu Ling remembered the room next to hers was empty, as was the room next to that. The people who'd lived in these rooms had vanished out of the blue, all of them apart from Kuan Kuan. In the last four years, she'd been with these people day and night; you could say they constituted her entire world. Now this world was collapsing.

As a child, she'd had a recurring dream in which everyone on earth disappeared, leaving her all alone. She'd walk down a street in the predawn dark, all the streetlights on, tiny droplets of dew condensing in the air. At the junction, she'd turn onto an alleyway, where she'd find a restaurant. On the counter was a tall steamer emitting white puffs. After examining a few steamer drawers, she'd choose one and bring it over to a table by the window. She'd pour herself tea from the steel pot on the table, take chopsticks from the caddy, and pick up a steamed bun. There was no one in the restaurant, but it had everything she needed. Without anyone rushing her, she didn't need to be anxious. Neither was anyone waiting for her to finish eating so they could order her to go do this or that. She could move at her own pace. The only time in her life she could focus on her food. She'd chew slowly, not even impatient to get through the dough to taste the filling.

In the dream, she believed she was the protagonist of this world, and other people were no more than furniture, sent by the heavens and just as easily returned. Only she was fully alive, every pore breathing, every moment full of thought. Of course, she understood how immature these ideas were, but the dream gave her a sense of dignity. In this dream, no matter how poor you were, you could be the main character, and even a king who possessed an entire city was so fragile he could vanish at any moment. Yu Ling once had good friends she'd now lost touch with. They never stopped moving on. Sometimes they took jobs and quit even before the end of the month, not because they were dissatisfied with the work or had found something better, they just wanted to keep moving. Yu Ling thought they might have the same dream she did, of everyone else vanishing. In real life, though, the people around you would never go away, and you could only make yourself disappear. Endlessly changing positions was a way for them to take control of their lives. It was the only way they could be protagonists.

Yu Ling had to admit that one of the more alluring aspects of Donghu's plan was that it involved him taking her away from this place, in a way there would be no coming back from. She was trapped here. But what by? The generous wages? A child she could get on with? The great inertia of life? Today you put a few cucumbers into a sealed jar, and your most important task tomorrow would be to make sure they'd pickled properly. Switch wardrobes around when the seasons change, make a dentist appointment for the kid. Many of the things you did today were in preparation for tomorrow; if tomorrow never came, you'd have wasted today. *I'll just stay one more year*, Yu Ling kept telling herself, each time taking action to shape her own life. Apart from the money she'd put away these last few years, she had nothing at all.

And now they were the ones who'd disappeared, the people who'd hovered around her, pressing down on her the whole time. When she chatted with other nannies, they invariably admitted they felt much more at ease when their employers weren't home. They longed for their sirs and ma'ams to go partying, get drunk, lose their way, take a lover. Every nanny adores an empty house. Yu Ling listened out when anyone walked past her room. As their footsteps drew near, her heart would clench. Then someone would shout her name, and no matter who it was, no matter what time, she had to call out in response and leave her room. There was a lock on her door, but she never used it. If they noticed her locking her door, they'd surely ask why. When she said her room was comfortable, she meant when there were no footsteps to be heard, like now. She thought about the goose. She ought to lock it up to avoid it shitting on the carpet. Then again—the carpet might be expensive, but what did that have to do with her?

At dawn, she went to the nursery, found Kuan Kuan's bed empty, went downstairs, and pulled open the tent flaps. He was sleeping peacefully, his arms flung around Teddy the elephant and a zebra. She made a few rounds of the house. No sign of the goose or its shit.

When she passed the main bedroom, she paused a moment at the door, then slammed it open. This crass action brought her glee. She strode into the room, enjoying its spaciousness. Sitting at the vanity, she pulled open the drawer. A lone jewelry case, forlorn in a corner. Why had Hui left it behind?

She picked up the midnight-blue velvet case. It didn't weigh much. She popped open the lid and a milk tooth tumbled out. Picking it up between two fingers, she squinted at it. She remembered it falling out at dinner, Kuan Kuan howling and bleeding from the mouth. She'd left the tooth on the table and taken the boy to get cleaned up. When they returned, the tooth was gone. She'd thought Qin Wen must have tossed it in the trash, which annoyed her. The custom where she came from was to place fallen teeth from the lower jaw somewhere high up, like the roof, to make sure the new tooth grew in quickly and evenly.

"Ah, there you are." Yu Ling put the tooth back on its velvet lining and snapped the case shut.

9

At seven, Yu Ling went to the kitchen as usual to prepare breakfast. From the fridge she took three eggs, a few mushrooms, and a packet of ham, ingredients for an omelet. Without Hui here, the kitchen felt much bigger—she liked having it to herself. Cooking was actually Hui's job, but Kuan Kuan didn't like her food, so what else could they do? Hui disagreed, naturally. To her, even Kuan Kuan's taste buds were in cahoots with Yu Ling. When they had to use the kitchen at the same time, each stuck to her own side, with the island as a border. Hui would use the stove, Yu Ling the oven. Hui liked frying things, while Yu Ling was into baking. Being Sichuanese, Hui put chilies in everything, which their sir enjoyed. Yu Ling's food was more Westernized, which Kuan Kuan and their ma'am preferred. This should have been fine—each of them in a different camp, satisfying different needs. But then Hui got the idea in her head that Yu Ling was learning how to cook Western style so the family would bring her along when they emigrated.

This theory had no basis in fact whatsoever, unless it was that whenever the subject of Kuan Kuan going to college abroad came up, the boy would say he wanted Yu Ling to come with him. But how could a kid's words be taken seriously?

Yu Ling had to admit that she'd first started Western cooking to please her ma'am, but quickly developed an interest of her own—although it was sometimes hard for her to tell if her passions were her own, or the result of other people's expectations. In any case, the conditions were ideal: every piece of equipment she might need, all sorts of Western cookbooks on the shelves, and a supermarket nearby that carried every ingredient mentioned in these books. "Wow, you read English? You must have done well at school," Hui had once said when she happened to see Yu Ling reading an American cookbook. Then, with a shake of her head and a sigh, "Not that it did you any good, you still ended up as a nanny."

Hui had always hated Yu Ling, which made sense. After all, Yu Ling was here first. When they listed their preferences at the agency, some people would specify they didn't want a household that already had a nanny. Although families with more than one helper were likely to be well-off, newcomers often got bullied by the senior nanny. Yu Ling never treated Hui badly, and looked the other way when she stole stuff, yet Hui still treated her like the enemy. Probably she'd claim this was a preemptive strike. In her imagination, Yu Ling was a villain who'd snatched Kuan Kuan from the arms of another nanny before squeezing her out.

That's not how it was, though—it was Yu Ling who got poached from a friend of Qin Wen's. Sometimes she wondered what her life would be like if she hadn't said yes to that offer. It was hard to imagine never knowing Kuan Kuan or meeting Donghu, yet she'd lived her whole life up till then without them, and been perfectly happy.

Her previous employer was a fortyish woman from Hong Kong, whose full name Yu Ling could no longer remember—she'd just called her Mrs. Wu. It was common for mainland nannies to call their ma'ams "Big Sister," in an attempt to make them feel closer, but the first time Yu Ling said "Big Sister Wu," her ma'am's face stiffened and she snapped, "Please call me Mrs. Wu." Turns out in Hong Kong it's the other way round: nannies are the ones who get called "sister." Mr. Wu was a Hong Konger too. They'd moved to the mainland a few years before and opened an interior design firm together. Qin Wen had hired Mrs. Wu to design her art studio and they quickly became friends. For a while, Qin Wen often visited their downtown penthouse, which was painted white from floor to ceiling and had a picture window in the living room through which they could watch glowing rivers of traffic on the elevated highways at night.

"I'd like to come live the city life too," Qin Wen once said, curled up on the off-white couch hugging a cushion. Hairs were straggling loose from her bun and curling around her face, as if she wanted to look like she'd been through hardship. She referred to Golden Lake Villas as "our village," and the way she described it made Yu Ling imagine she lived in some remote part of the countryside. Mrs. Wu soon disabused her. "Don't trust a word Qin Wen says, she always thinks the grass is greener. She even asked if you'd be interested in cleaning her studio. I said you weren't looking for a new job. You're not, are you?"

Yu Ling shook her head.

It was true, she hadn't wanted a new position. The most satisfying thing about her current life was she didn't look like someone whose job was just "cleaning." The Wus had no children and enjoyed living simply. There wasn't much for Yu Ling to do, and she was usually done with her chores by morning. In the afternoon, she went to their office, where she sorted through catalogs and samples from houseware companies, and made phone calls to suppliers. She had even started learning basic Photoshop skills, such as changing the size and format of images. While she was there, she behaved just like everyone else: eating boxed lunches, drinking milk tea, doing overtime. Mrs. Wu treated her the same as her other employees, and she began to feel as if she actually worked there. Perhaps she'd eventually be able to get a real job as a designer's assistant. Her lack of education meant there was no way she could apply for such a position in the outside world, which meant her only shot was for one of her bosses to take a shine to her. She was thirty years old. Apart from hoping to get married and have children, she also longed to find a place for herself in this world. She definitely didn't want to be a nanny all her life.

How had she caught Qin Wen's eye? It was a mystery. All she'd ever done was serve tea and fruit to Qin Wen; they hadn't even spoken. Then Mrs. Wu said Qin Wen had formally requested that Yu Ling come clean her studio. Yu Ling asked, "And if I refuse?" Mrs. Wu sighed and said, "If you don't go, I won't be able to keep you here either. I can't afford to go against her. Do you understand?" Yu Ling looked down and said, "I thought I was helpful to you." Mrs. Wu said distractedly, "It's true, you're very capable." She sounded as if this meant nothing compared to the problem Yu Ling was causing her.

"But I can still refuse, can't I?" said Yu Ling.

"Of course. You have more freedom than us."

Yu Ling believed that. She thought she had the power to take the initiative. Then Qin Wen offered her a forty percent pay rise, and she realized there was no way to say no.

Now Yu Ling beat the eggs in a white porcelain bowl, then added milk and a pinch of pink salt. The chopped mushrooms and ham went into the frying pan first, then the egg mixture. She'd made omelets in this way since Kuan Kuan was four. He hated the earthy taste of raw mushrooms and would spit them out, but it was fine if they were stir-fried. Sometimes Yu Ling would sneak in a small amount of cooked carrot. Kuan Kuan was very picky, so she felt gratified whenever she saw he'd cleaned his plate. This was different from the satisfaction of having finished all her tasks and being able to sit down, it was more the sense that she was needed, that she couldn't be replaced. The manager of the agency was fond of saying, "Make sure you never think there's anything special about you." He wanted all the nannies to remember that if they took even one step out of line, there'd be someone waiting to take their place. Yet there was Qin Wen, offering so much more money, insisting on hiring her away. That was enough, she'd thought, to prove the manager wrong.

10

Kuan Kuan wandered into the kitchen rubbing his eyes.

Yu Ling glanced at him. "I told you not to sleep in the tent. You'll catch a cold."

"Where's the swan? I think I dreamed about it." Kuan Kuan ran out into the yard.

"Put on your coat!" Yu Ling yelled after him.

She folded the omelet over and slid it onto a plate, then poured some milk into a pan for the oatmeal. Once the oats were soft, she liked to add a spoonful of rice wine, some beaten egg, a few red dates, a handful of black sesame seeds. She glanced out the window to make sure Kuan Kuan had his coat on. The oatmeal came to a boil and she turned off the heat. A thick, milky fragrance settled over the room.

One summer evening four years ago, she'd arrived at the studio and found Qin Wen waiting for her. This was a large structure consisting of a workroom, reception room, and bedroom around an open-air siheyuan courtyard, strewn with stone urns from which lilies bloomed. Qin Wen called this place "my own little kingdom." Her plan was to come here each day to paint, because her kid raised such a ruckus she couldn't get anything done at her home studio. Yu Ling's job would be to keep this place clean and make her lunch. When Qin Wen went home in the evening, Yu Ling would be done for the day. The bedroom was hers—she would live here. Qin Wen was friendly, but never explained why she'd wanted to poach her in the first place. Finally, Yu Ling had to ask the question.

"Mrs. Wu mentioned that you're good with your hands and know how to stretch a canvas and paint with gouache. That's exactly what I need. How did you learn all that?"

"I used to work in a cloisonné painting place." Yu Ling looked down at the picture on the easel. "Do you mainly do portraits?"

"Alice Neel said 'portrait' is a word you use to flatter the sitter, they ought to be called 'pictures of people.'" Qin Wen took a couple of steps back to examine Yu Ling. "I could paint one of you."

She went over to the bookshelf and pulled out a catalog. "Look, isn't she amazing?" Paintings of men, women, children, animals, all thickly outlined in black, so crudely rendered a small child could have drawn them. Yu Ling couldn't see what was so great about these.

"Do you know why Alice Neel liked drawing mothers and children so much? It's because she abandoned her own child." Qin Wen studied a picture of a woman and her daughter. "Art always begins with loss."

And yet Qin Wen's art invariably started with gaining something. In order to bring herself closer to Alice Neel, she had to acquire one of her paintings. A year later, she nabbed one at auction and hung it in the living room.

As for the picture of Yu Ling, it took more than a year to complete. The artist always had something more urgent to depict: a pregnant woman, a pair of twin girls, a birthday party clown. Only when Qin Wen was done with these, or at least done being interested in them, would she return to Yu Ling. Eventually, she finished the work she titled *Woman, Seated*. Yu Ling was disappointed: she found the woman in the picture much uglier than herself. Shoulders hunched, hands clasped, apparently anxious about something—perhaps the fact of being seated. Just being there, not doing anything, left her ill at ease. What most annoyed Yu Ling was the sluggish blankness in the woman's gaze. Her eyeballs looked like buttons fastened in their sockets, completely immobile. Qin Wen was delighted with the result, though. She said it was the closest she'd come to Alice Neel's work. When she had her exhibition, she promised Yu Ling, this would take pride of place. Yu Ling worried to start with, then realized no one would have any idea who this "woman, seated" was.

Apart from the fuss about this picture, the rest of their time together was quite happy. Her ma'am was always gleeful when she arrived, like a schoolgirl playing hooky. As Qin Wen worked, Yu Ling would be off to one side mixing paints, sorting catalogs, or stretching canvases. At first she was careful not to make any noise, then she discovered Qin Wen actually didn't like quiet as she painted. If Yu Ling was silent for too long, Qin Wen would ask her to say something. Not knowing what to talk about, Yu Ling would tell stories from her child-hood: climbing trees to steal eggs, making rafts from car tires, trapping mice with her little brother to prank the village head-man's wife with. Qin Wen always burst out laughing at these anecdotes, which made Yu Ling think she enjoyed them. After all, she often said things like "It's so nice having you here with me." Yet when Qin Wen later described this part of her life to friends, they were invariably "days of utter solitude." Qin Wen soon understood this utter solitude didn't actually help her pro-duce better work, but rather turned her "own little kingdom" into a form of self-inflicted punishment. She began inviting friends to keep her company. These elegantly dressed women would sit by the window facing the courtyard, animatedly chat-ting about the latest openings, that season's auctions, the jew-elry designers they'd just discovered. Easy jazz played on the turntable, and the air was perfumed with the aroma of pour-over coffee. If only there was a little dessert, the ladies would say, preferably something freshly baked. And so Qin Wen en-couraged Yu Ling to start baking.

"Our cake was a big hit, they didn't leave a single crumb." Even if Qin Wen's fingers hadn't touched a speck of flour, she would still say "our cake." Yu Ling had no problem with this, in fact it made her proud. She liked hearing Qin Wen say "our," as if they had many things in common, these many things comprising the vast amount Qin Wen possessed and Yu Ling's modicum. "Our" was where she most wanted to be, a little stream flowing into the ocean.

Yu Ling became a lot busier after Qin Wen started receiving guests in her studio. She had to serve the ladies coffee and snacks, make simple meals, organize small salons, even help with the decor beforehand. She realized she was good at these things, and the visitors invariably praised her. By being immersed in these high-class activities, she felt she was learning many things. If not for Kuan Kuan, she and Qin Wen would probably have continued to get on like a house on fire.

No one could say why the child developed such a strong attachment to her. Yu Ling was only meant to take over for a week from his nanny, who'd gone back home for a family emergency. In that short space of time, the boy grew so fond of her, he refused to let her go. For all that she looked stern and didn't know many games, he adored her, and would cling to her legs like a little cat. When Qin Wen forced them apart and drove Yu Ling back to the studio, Kuan Kuan ran out into the cold in just his pajamas, chasing after the car. That evening he developed a high fever but refused to take any medicine until Qin Wen brought Yu Ling back.

"I really need you, but I have to let him have you, because the child's wishes come first. I have no choice," said Qin Wen. She didn't act like it, though. At times she'd abruptly send Yu Ling out on some errand, and Kuan Kuan would burst out sobbing when he couldn't find her. Or else she'd insist on bringing Kuan Kuan out herself, buying him all sorts of toys to make him admit that his mama treated him better than anyone else. Once Yu Ling began taking care of Kuan Kuan, Qin Wen began blowing hot and cold, and their relationship grew patchy. In the meantime, Yu Ling and Kuan Kuan became fonder of each other by the day. When Yu Ling thought about how she'd have to part with Kuan Kuan someday, a quiet sadness would overtake her, and she'd have to remind herself that she was meant to be taking action to shape her own life.

Breakfast was getting cold. Yu Ling called for the boy to come inside and eat. She poured him a glass of milk, and hot tea for herself. The boy sliced open the omelet to inspect it for anything he didn't like, and breathed a sigh of relief to find no carrots. He looked up and stared at Yu Ling in some astonishment.

"You're sitting in Ma's place."

"Am I?" said Yu Ling. "Stop tearing that omelet apart and just eat it."

11

The clock showed eight. Normally they'd be almost at the school by this time. Yu Ling stood outside the tent, hollering Kuan Kuan's name.

"I have a fever," said the boy weakly, sticking his head out.

"I'll take your temperature."

"I mean, I predict I'm about to have a fever."

"I don't know how to call in sick because of a prediction. I'll phone Miss Amy and you can tell her yourself."

"No!" Kuan Kuan coughed a few times. "My throat hurts. I can't speak."

"Then which little dog do I hear barking?"

Kuan Kuan clapped both hands over his mouth and retreated into the tent. Yu Ling decided to let him be. She didn't feel strongly about sending him to school, partly because she wasn't sure if she should pretend nothing had happened. His teacher might well have seen the news, and Yu Ling would look stupid if she dropped the boy off as usual, urging him to eat his vegetables and stay hydrated, probably as stupid as Miss Amy thought she was anyway. But if she didn't want to appear stupid, she'd have to submit to Miss Amy's interrogation and spill everything she knew.

"Oh my goodness, what is the world coming to?" this young woman, who'd just returned from studying in England, would exclaim whenever she heard bad news, shaking her head, naive eyes open wide, as if the world were a disappointing pupil. Within her dismay was a kernel of superiority, as if to say: *Everything has been ruined by you people.* And who did *you people* include? Yu Ling wasn't sure, but she felt implicated. That's why, one time, when she overheard a parent commenting on a news story about a man who'd broken his wife's ribs during a fight, Yu Ling said, "This sort of thing happens all the time, what's the big deal?" Miss Amy had stared at her in shock, as if she was some kind of monster.

Never mind who the monster was, Yu Ling knew that if Miss Amy were aware of Kuan Kuan's situation, she'd definitely step in. After just one day of life without her ma'am, would Yu Ling be expected to take orders from this young lady?

Yu Ling tidied up the kitchen and went to sit by the window with a cup of warm water. All was silent, and only by staring at the bamboo leaves outside could she imagine she heard a faint breeze rustling. For a moment, she felt she and Kuan Kuan were the only human beings left in the world. This was nice to start with, but she quickly grew uneasy. It was impossible to stop herself imagining what was going on elsewhere. What would Donghu's next step be? Had Qin Wen been arrested?

Was Kuan Kuan's grandmother conscious yet? She sensed unseen danger, like a rumbling deep beneath the earth's crust, rushing upward from a great distance away. And no one knew it was coming. This thought made the quiet of the house suddenly unbearable. She grabbed her phone. Less than two minutes later, Miss Amy called.

"Oh dear, poor Kuan Kuan. I hope he feels better soon. Is his ma at home? Her phone is off. Could you ask her to give me a call?"

"I don't know where she is."

"And his ba?" Miss Amy didn't sound like she was being disingenuous.

"He's not home either." *At least I'm not lying,* Yu Ling told herself.

"Could you ask his ma to get in touch when she's home?" A pause. "It's like this, Nanny Yu, the school rules say that only parents can call in sick for a child. We had a situation where the nanny was taking her kid out for a whole day, and the parents had no idea. I know you'd never do such a thing, I just wanted to explain why we have these rules."

After hanging up, Yu Ling remembered why she'd hated Miss Amy from the beginning. On the first day of school, she'd overheard Miss Amy saying to a parent, "I don't plan to have children of my own, that would be selfish. I want to give all my love to my students instead." What hypocrisy. Someone who truly loved kids would never say such a thing. She just didn't want to make sacrifices, and this was the excuse she'd seized upon. God help the man who married her. A couple of months later, while picking up Kuan Kuan, she'd seen a ring on Miss Amy's fourth finger. A thin silvery band with a diamond, smallish but very brilliant.

Yu Ling looked at her phone. No word from Donghu. She found it hard to imagine he'd have given up just like that. Maybe he was brewing a new plan. She felt a shiver of unease and decided to try calling Hu Yafei's family in Guangxi again.

Kuan Kuan dashed in to grab his green chenille kiddie chair and dragged it outside. When Yu Ling shouted at him, he replied with exaggerated sign language, looking smug at having remembered to keep up his sore-throat ruse. He could still hear, though, and she didn't want him listening in on her call. She went out to the backyard.

No one answered the first time. She tried again, and after a long while, the same woman as yesterday picked up, her voice even raspier. "Hold on, I'll call you back from a different number."

Yu Ling sat on the gazebo's long bench, phone in her hand. Whenever they had visitors, her sir would bring them out here. He was very proud of this gazebo, which nestled amid the landscape. This was the best view in the whole garden, with a pond to one side, porous Taihu rocks directly ahead, and the teahouse farther back, the calligraphy "Chrysanthemum by the Creek" visible through the window, wreathed with steam if the kettle was on the stove. If you sat at the other end of the bench, you'd see instead Qin Wen's workspace in the sunroom, easels draped with velvet. The bench on the other side of the gazebo offered a completely different view. This was known as a shifting landscape, scenery that transformed with your every move.

The phone call didn't come. Yu Ling left the gazebo and began watering the magnolia tree with a hose. So much of the garden had been paved over that not much water actually reached its roots, and its trunk remained slender. It kept getting taller, but its branches shrank inward, like the ribs of a broken umbrella. Her sir found it aesthetically lacking, and had said he would get rid of it if it was still in this condition come the summer. "We'll give it one more spring," he'd said.

Yu Ling wished she could tell him it wouldn't be like this if the lawn were still in place. When she'd first arrived, the garden was mostly grass, with no other plants beyond a few rosebushes against the wall. She saw a lot of potential here, and asked Qin Wen if she could plant some flowers to save buying them from the market. "Can you grow hydrangeas?" Qin Wen had asked. "I like the blue ones." Yu Ling had said of course she could. One drizzly morning, she returned with a large bag of seeds, including three types of hydrangeas, plus two varieties each of peonies and tulips. The seller threw in some tomato and strawberry seeds. White strawberries, he'd said.

A week after she'd planted the seeds, a well-drilled team of laborers showed up. Within a day, they'd uprooted the entire lawn and replaced it with paving stones sourced from an ancestral hall in Shanxi. "Go look around. Which rich folk do you see with grass in their yards?" said her sir. "Every slab of this stone comes with its own history. What history does grass have?" Next, the work team hoisted in several Taihu rocks. One of them, spindly as a skeleton, was chosen as the centerpiece, the first thing you saw when you entered—like the saying "Open the gates and see the mountain." The gazebo had been shipped here from an ancient mansion in Huizhou, and the pine trees had once grown by the entrance of a Kyoto temple. The only flowering trees were the magnolia and a crab apple, because a profusion of flowers would have been vulgar, bereft of classical beauty. The day the construction was done, her sir threw a big party, and hung a calligraphy board over the garden gate that read "Hall of the Expansive Heart."

Yu Ling was upset about that lawn for a very long time, and didn't like going into the yard. The rocks and gazebo felt frigid to her, like the concubines' palace garden she'd seen on TV. The maids in those historical dramas never came to good ends, always hanging themselves or jumping into wells.

The phone rang. An unknown number. She answered.

"Where's Donghu? Why isn't he answering his phone?" The voice had such a strong accent, it took her a second to make out what he was saying. Then she realized: this was Donghu's roommate, Dalei.

"Did something go wrong with the transaction?" Dalei said quietly. When Yu Ling didn't answer, he went on, "Don't try to lie. I loaned him that van, and I've been paying his rent for the last two months. I'm part of whatever scheme you two cooked up."

"The whole thing's a bust. Leave the kid alone."

"What kid? Wasn't it a stone? What's with the stone, was it fake?"

Yu Ling said she had no idea what Donghu was up to, but Dalei didn't believe her. He insisted she was the mastermind. Donghu had told him he'd gambled and won a piece of jade from a mine in Yunnan, and he planned to sell it to the family

Yu Ling worked for, only he was afraid it would get swapped out along the way, so he was going to transport it himself.

"So tell me, did something go wrong?"

Yu Ling hung up without answering. Donghu had moved into the apartment in the eastern suburbs just three months ago. She'd only heard him mention Dalei a couple of times, complaining that he was always coming home in the middle of the night because he worked so far away, waking Donghu up. There actually had been a piece of jade—Donghu had borrowed money from a loan shark to buy it—but that was a year ago.

She looked up at the gazebo roof, zooming in on a groove in one of the rafters. There it was, a black sphere about the size of a walnut, just like the one in the study. Now she believed Donghu: there were cameras everywhere, hidden in places they wouldn't be seen. Her every move was being filmed. Right away she thought: *Wouldn't they have caught Hui stealing?* If anyone was looking for the missing items, the evidence was there. Evidence of what? Hui's guilt, or Yu Ling's innocence? She realized how much anxiety she'd been holding on to that she would be blamed. Now here was proof that she hadn't done anything wrong. Also, if anyone climbed the garden wall, they'd come into range of this camera. Hadn't Donghu said these were being monitored constantly? Yu Ling looked up at the watchful sphere above her and felt protected.

12

D on't call the other number again, understand?" The Guangxi woman called that afternoon, from a different phone. She said someone had rung that number the day before to inform them of Hu Yafei's arrest, with instructions that the grandmother should take care of the child. This made the woman suspect that number was bugged. Yu Ling didn't understand—what was there to keep secret? They were only discussing how to get the child to Guangxi. The woman didn't give her a chance to ask questions. Her voice sounded very fragile as she explained that Kuan Kuan's grandmother was out of danger, but her blood vessels were seriously blocked, and she remained unconscious.

"I suppose Kuan Kuan's mother hasn't come back," said the woman confidently. "She must be in hiding. Lucky for her. Or maybe she had wind of this."

Yu Ling asked how long she would stay hidden.

"Who the hell knows how long this whole thing will take?"

growled the woman. "Hong Kong isn't safe either. She'll probably find a way to get to the States."

Yu Ling said she wouldn't abandon Kuan Kuan.

"I'll bet you anything you like that she won't be back."

"Who's going to take care of the kid, then?"

"We could do it, but it's not convenient for us to come to Beijing right now, understand? The case is still being investigated, and no one knows what's going to happen next. If you really insist, you could send him to Nanning."

Yu Ling wanted to ask what "really insist" meant.

"If you send the child here, of course we'll take care of him. But we can't fetch him ourselves, understand? Do you know how to buy a plane ticket? Do you have money?"

Talking to her as if she'd only just arrived in the big city. Huffily, Yu Ling replied that yes, she did know how. The woman gave her an address and hung up.

She ought to get Kuan Kuan to Nanning as soon as possible. The woman had sounded reluctant, but they were his family. Besides, as long as the boy was here, Donghu wouldn't give up his plan.

She thought of Donghu standing by the door, saying, "I do want to make a go of it with you," arms by his sides, looking chastened as a child who'd done something wrong. Ever since the loan shark had come looking for him, he'd been ducking here and there, frequently moving house.

When she saw the shovel the day before, Yu Ling felt she and Donghu were finished. Then overnight she'd forgiven him. She felt something drawing their relationship closer. It was innocence, she decided. They'd almost placed themselves in serious trouble but, thanks to a series of mishaps, had avoided any guilt. Innocence meant freedom, an abstract concept that became real when she imagined her ma'am on the run. Freedom was a picnic beneath the sun, taking big bites out of a beef skewer. If they ran out of Wagyu, she'd have Mongolian beef instead. She dialed Donghu's number. She decided to tell him she no longer blamed him, to make a plan for what to do next. She was happy to pay off part of his debt with her savings. But all she got was a recorded message: his phone was off. Maybe he was avoiding Dalei. Why would he want to keep the van, though? She tried again later and got the same message.

She made Kuan Kuan udon for lunch, but only managed to eat a little herself. Afterward, she distracted herself with housework. She changed the sheets, washed her and Kuan Kuan's clothes, and cleaned the carpets. Through the roar of the vacuum cleaner, she faintly heard Qin Xinwei's name coming from the living room. Or perhaps she didn't actually hear the words, and it was more a shift in tone when this part of the news bulletin arrived, a lowering of the voice that she was becoming extremely familiar with. Sure enough, Kuan Kuan was holding the remote, turning to Yu Ling with a look of sheer confusion, gesturing at the screen as if he were still in sign language mode. Yu Ling told him to go do something meaningful, drawing or piano practice, otherwise she'd send him back to school. The boy stuck out his tongue, dropped the remote, and scampered off.

When Yu Ling looked back at the screen, there was an older man in a gray suit, white shirt, and dark blue tie. She startled, thinking for a moment this was Qin Xinwei—which made sense, he was at the center of this affair, of course they would interview him. She thought of journalists as all-powerful, able to speak with anyone from foreign presidents to death row inmates. She'd once seen a program about condemned prisoners, and was surprised to find them meekly, forthrightly answering the presenter's questions, as if they were telling someone else's story. Maybe this was a rehearsal for leaving themselves. Now her fingers twisted together with tension as she stared at the man, waiting for him to repent. Donghu had said he faced life imprisonment. She didn't think it would be that serious, but no matter what, he wasn't going to be executed.

No, that wasn't Qin Xinwei. She realized her error before he'd even opened his mouth. He was dressed similarly, down to the same hairstyle, and when he spoke he sounded the same too, but there was nothing repentant in his tone. He sounded confident, even pleased with himself. Script in hand, arms resting on the table, firmly planted in his seat, with absolutely no wish to depart from himself.

"We all feel shaken by Comrade Qin Xinwei's situation. It hurts us deeply," said the man in conclusion, looking up at the camera.

She tried again in the afternoon, but Donghu's phone was still off.

Two people came to the door that day. The first was Mr. Sun, the main fruit-and-veg supplier to Golden Lake Villas, from his organic farm. Yu Ling pulled open the plastic cover to look at his wares and said they wouldn't be needing any more arugula or kale.

"Has Ms. Qin Wen stopped eating salads?"

"Give me some zucchini and mustard greens instead. Do you have bean sprouts?"

"No, those are cultivated in water, and customers suspected they weren't natural enough. I can get you fresh-picked strawberries tomorrow, and there'll be cherries in a few days." Before leaving, Mr. Sun asked her to remind her ma'am that their account was empty and needed to be topped up.

The vegetables in front of her now looked unspeakably precious. Yu Ling carefully wrapped them and put them in the fridge. With what was already in there, they had enough for about a week. She tried Donghu again, to no avail. She stared into space for a while, then decided to make herself a cup of tea and pulled open the bottommost kitchen drawer, where an array of colorful tea bags stood in neat rows, like a library card catalog. Sometimes she treated them like a fortune-telling: She'd think of a color and pick one with her eyes shut. If the tea bag in her hand matched the one in her mind, that meant good luck was coming her way. But today she thought of red and got blue, exactly what she didn't want. She was holding the pouch of Lady Grey, wondering if there was a way she could somehow connect it to red, when the doorbell rang.

At the door was Duomei, a nanny from a block away on Rose Street, on her way home with the little girl she looked after, who was in first grade at Kuan Kuan's school.

"Miss Amy asked me to check in on the family." Duomei stuck her head in to investigate. The little girl stood in the doorway until Duomei nudged her, at which point she sprinted into the house like a mechanical doll prodded into motion.

"Kuan Kuan, Kuan Kuan!"

Duomei tried to follow the girl into the house, but Yu Ling stepped into her path.

"I told Miss Amy not to worry. We treat children the same whether or not their parents are around." Duomei favored colorful leggings; today's were moss green. "I heard about what happened to Kuan Kuan's grandpa, and his father was taken too. That only leaves his mother, and she won't get very far." Duomei stepped closer and whispered, "That makes you happy, doesn't it?"

Yu Ling stared at her. "Why would I be happy?"

"Hui told me some stuff," said Duomei, shrugging. "It doesn't matter. Most people around here loathe your ma'am, you know. That whole thing about restricting dog-walking hours, that was all her, wasn't it? She single-handedly rigged the neighborhood committee vote. It's her fault our golden retriever never gets to see the sun! I've heard estate management even consulted her about what trees to plant by the lake. Who does she think she is, the Baroness Thatcher of Golden Lake Villas?" Duomei tried to look past Yu Ling into the house. "Of course, it's a pity about the kid. What are you and Hui planning to do?"

Yu Ling told her Hui had left the day before. Duomei immediately understood Hui must have taken a bunch of valuables, and said this was perfectly normal. She knew a nanny who'd emptied the entire safe when she left, because she understood her ma'am so well that she knew the combination would be her husband's and son's birthdays put together.

"The more you care about something, the more dangerous

it is to you," said Duomei in conclusion. She stared at Yu Ling weirdly. "What's up with you?"

Yu Ling looked like she was choking. Tears were glistening in her eyes, and she was pounding at her chest. "Nothing. You're completely right."

The little girl ran back over and took Duomei's hand. "Nanny, Kuan Kuan's turned into a mute."

13

A password is a special language you use when speaking to a computer. The computer doesn't understand words, yet some people insist on using human language. Yu Ling was one of them. She knew the most secure thing was to let the computer generate a random string of letters, numbers, and symbols. When she did this, though, the lack of order made her fearful, as if she'd fallen into a completely illogical dream. She knew she didn't need to memorize that string of nonsense, but what if something went wrong with the computer? Better to come up with her own.

Even if you invent your own password, that doesn't mean you have to use birthdays. Many people make up a number, keeping things simple. Yu Ling wasn't one of those people. There are those who see birthdays as just arbitrary numbers, not worth celebrating. Does a carton of milk celebrate its own production date? Yu Ling wasn't one of those people either. She treated her birth date as a lucky number. If she happened to come upon those digits, that was a sign of good fortune. For instance, if she went to the bank and her queue number was her birthday, that meant she was going to earn more money in the coming year. Naturally, what good luck looked like wasn't always so straightforward, but on these occasions she felt the heavens smiling down at her.

Yet she rarely used her birth date as a password. Firstly, because that would be too easy to guess. Secondly, if she were to turn her password into a prayer, it should be a complete thought. "Wish me happiness" is still missing something, only "Wish me happiness with such-and-such" is a full blessing.

Last New Year, neither Yu Ling nor Donghu went back to their respective hometowns. She needed to make New Year's Eve dinner for Kuan Kuan's family, and he was driving a delivery of fresh flowers from Yunnan to the western suburbs, where a resort needed them for its holiday display. He'd been unable to find steady work since he got fired. Apart from gambling and trafficking precious stones, he'd picked up a few gigs from a trucker message board. The two of them agreed to celebrate the New Year together. Yu Ling invited him over. Many families at Golden Lake Villas would be setting off fireworks, the sort that filled the entire sky with their brilliance.

That afternoon, Hu Yafei invited two families to visit, which meant Kuan Kuan had playmates. Yu Ling was busy in the kitchen while Donghu was speeding along in his van of fresh flowers with a full tank of gas. They called each other every now and then to share what they were up to. Yu Ling said she'd just killed a lobster, but even chopped in two, the critter was still twitching. Donghu said he'd gone through a tunnel illuminated murky green like something from a horror film. An hour later, Yu Ling said she was making chicken soup with fish maw, then had to describe what fish maw looked like. "Chopped-up lengths of garden hose." Donghu said he'd reached the hotel and was waiting for them to sign for the delivery. "Is it nice there?" asked Yu Ling. Donghu said it was okay, maybe a bit deserted, there weren't many guests. "That's a waste of flowers, then," said Yu Ling.

Donghu phoned again as Yu Ling was making dumplings, to say he was lost. He'd reached a dead end on an unlit road, and one of his headlights wasn't working. "That's just my luck. The year's ending and I still don't get to have one day when nothing goes wrong!" He pounded the steering wheel, setting off the horn. After a while, the earsplitting racket stopped, and she thought he'd hung up, but then she heard a quiet sobbing. She tilted her head to one side, clamping the phone to her shoulder as she worked, listening to him cry. Sorrow welled up from deep within his throat. They'd been together for over a year, and she'd never seen him so vulnerable. Kuan Kuan and the other kids ran into the dining room, covering up his weeping with their cacophony. Yu Ling rinsed the flour off her hands and walked over to the window, holding her phone in one hand and resting the other against the sill, letting it take some of her weight. She couldn't stand this. Hearing men cry was unbearably painful. It felt as if she was listening to something tear apart inside their bodies. Some things, once broken, can never be repaired.

"It's okay, it's okay," she said softly. "I promise I'll leave here with you."

They both knew what she meant by "leave here with you." They'd half joked about this plan many times, in that it was a joke to her but not to Donghu. He desperately needed to pay off the loan sharks, and this scheme was him clutching at straws. She might not have agreed to go along with it, but she'd made him confident that he could get the money from this wealthy family. She'd done this to keep Donghu by her side, and fantasizing about this evil plan was a way of venting her feelings. But on that New Year's Eve, listening to Donghu's heartbreaking sobs, she realized how cruel she'd been. She was partly responsible for this irreversible sundering that was happening inside him.

By the time Donghu got to Golden Lake Villas, it was nearly two in the morning. He parked outside and she walked him in. Red lanterns hung along both sides of the street, and the air was thick with the sulfurous reek of gunpowder. A light snow fell, the bright flakes disappearing into the pine trees. She dragged the exhausted Donghu in a jog to the front door. They went into the garden through the garage, down a stone-flagged path to the wine cellar.

It wasn't particularly warm here, but otherwise perfect. Soft lighting, a comfortable leather couch, countless bottles of wine. They took one from the rack at random and opened it. Yu Ling went to the kitchen and came back with two plates of dumplings, along with a jar of the pickled garlic she'd been steeping in vinegar for the last two weeks.

The steam rising off the food moistened Donghu's eyes, making his lashes look exceptionally lush. "From now on, we'll be two people, one heart." He raised his crystal glass high, as if it were a trophy. After a few more drinks, they rolled around on the sheepskin rug. His body was broad and sturdy as a stove, and kept away the damp, cold air around them.

On the fifth of the new year, Yu Ling opened an account at a different bank and transferred her savings there, because Donghu said once they'd carried out their plan, Hu Yafei might go to the bank he paid her wages into and get them to freeze her account. That day, she emerged from the bank into the harsh winter sunlight, and called Donghu to say it was done. She couldn't resist adding that the PIN was both their birthdays. With Donghu being part of it, it was a complete blessing.

"Whose birthday did you put first?" asked Donghu.

After Duomei left, Yu Ling went back to the dining room. The blue tea bag was still on the table. How prominent the blue now looked. She ripped open the packaging and brewed herself some tea. Pulling out a stool, she sat at the kitchen island and logged into her bank account on her phone. The balance was ¥207.40. For once, the bank wasn't enthusiastically mobbing her with a whole range of wealth management options. The page was sparse. She was free to do whatever she wanted with this ¥207.40.

The transfer had taken place the night before, at 9:51 p.m. That must have been just after they got back, when Donghu was fiddling with her phone. And when he told her to keep her phone off, that was to stop her from receiving an alert from her bank. She turned this over in her mind. Apart from the change in her role, Donghu had basically carried out his scheme as planned, fleeing through the night once he had his hands on the cash. For all she knew, he was following the route he'd outlined: the bus to Wuhan, from where he'd travel to Yunnan, where the locals he'd met gambling on jade could help him find a place to stay, then across the border into Myanmar. He'd sworn to Yu Ling that as long as they could reach Yunnan, there was nothing to worry about. She didn't actually know who would have helped them in Yunnan, or where they would have gone. He'd mentioned Dali, and also Ruili. She'd thought at the time that Ruili must be a district of Dali, but looking at the map now, she saw they were very far apart.

She stared at the map, as if waiting for a place-name to jump out at her and tell her Donghu was there. After a while, she realized she didn't particularly care to know Donghu's whereabouts, and closed the app. Yesterday she'd been an accomplice, today a victim. Donghu had swung his fist but didn't manage to hit anyone, until her face got in the way. Just as well, she suddenly thought, hadn't she planned to give him the money anyway? She'd promised it to him in her mind, it was just that she hadn't had the chance to say it out loud. And now the money had eased Donghu's difficulties, that could be an end to the matter. If she'd been willing to do this from the beginning, perhaps they wouldn't have needed to go on that "spring outing" in the first place. Back then, she'd been so certain there could only be one use for the money: their marital home. She'd been so focused on marriage, even thinking it was more important than Kuan Kuan's safety. She thought back to the rope and ether in Donghu's van. The clang of the shovel against the hard earth. Compared to that horrifying outcome, losing a few years' savings was no big deal. A necessary sacrifice, a curb on her unhealthy desires. Now she could clearly see what she hadn't been able to accept before: she and Donghu would never have been happily married, he'd only have dragged her into ever greater danger. And yet she missed his burly body, the way his strong arms folded her into his chest, sturdy like a home that would never collapse.

Yu Ling dunked the tea bag in her mug to extract the last bits of flavor, then tossed it in the trash. She needed to think up a new PIN to protect her last ¥207.40.

14

The boy slept in the tent again. By the time Yu Ling came downstairs, he was awake and sitting by the opening, ripping pages from Qin Wen's fashion magazines and folding them into airplanes. An entire fleet stood waiting, ready for war games.

"Are you still not talking?" Yu Ling went into the kitchen.

The boy followed her and asked timidly, "Do I have to go to school today?"

"No, you can stay here. I'm going out to take care of some things."

The boy blinked. "I'd like some Rongji pastries."

"That's out of my way."

"Can Uncle Dong chauffeur you?"

"He's on vacation."

"Auntie Hui?"

"She had to go home. Family stuff."

"Stop lying, I know what's going on," said the boy. "Everyone's going out to have fun because Ma and Ba aren't home."

Yu Ling crouched to look him in the eye. "Do you want to have some fun too? How about going somewhere with hills and water? You could go on a spring outing every day."

Kuan Kuan didn't look up from the paper airplane he was folding, running his fingernail back and forth along a crease. Yu Ling told him about going to Nanning. His grandma was ill, she said, and his ba was still away on a business trip, so he wanted the boy to go visit his grandma. This sounded ridiculous, she knew. They hadn't seen each other for a couple of years, and Kuan Kuan's faint memories of his grandmother weren't enough of a hook to hang this plan on.

"Spring outing every day? Great! I'll go if you go." He flipped the plane over and raised it high. "Look, it's a Mama 747!"

The plane had very broad wings but a narrow nose, more like a crane's beak. On one of the wings was half of Qin Wen's face: straight black bangs, high cheekbones, eyes wider and more vivacious than in real life. Yu Ling recognized this photo: it was part of a feature on "women collectors" in a lifestyle magazine. On the day of the shoot, Qin Wen had agonized over what to wear before settling on a loose smoky-blue cotton top treated to cover its surface with hundreds of tiny wrinkles, her hair scraped back into a bun. "I want to show my artistic side," she said. Then the article came out and she exploded in rage, claiming the photographer had made her look like a textile factory girl.

The boy took a few steps back and launched the Mama 747, which made a few loops before plunging to the floor. He picked it up gingerly and crimped the tail a few times to increase its heft, then weighed it in his palm to make sure the wings were even.

"Do you miss your mama?" Yu Ling heard herself say in a severe voice.

"No!" The boy flung the door open and ran out into the yard.

After breakfast, Yu Ling went to the front gate to ask Lu, the security guard, to call the secondhand electronics dealer. The man showed up half an hour later, and Yu Ling showed him the spare TV set. It had only been used a few times before getting relegated to the cellar when a new model arrived. The dealer could see she was desperate and offered a very low price, which she only realized later, when she looked up flights and couldn't afford any of them. The Guangxi woman's concern hadn't been groundless. Yu Ling had flown before, but it was always her sir's assistant who booked the tickets. Of course, it wouldn't be too difficult for her to learn how to do it, but then she got stressed thinking about getting through security. Didn't they scrutinize every item in your bag and pat you up and down? What if they found something she shouldn't have brought and detained her?

Instead, she bought two train tickets for that evening. It would take a full twenty-four hours to get there. She packed a suitcase with just two sets of clothes for herself, filling the rest with Kuan Kuan's things. He wanted to bring the goose, but she told him birds weren't allowed on the train. He insisted she find a way, and it took a lot of energy to convince him that the goose would be safer and happier here.

Kuan Kuan was most concerned about whether the goose would be able to come and go freely. He wanted it to be able to rest in Swan Home whenever it wanted, even though it hadn't actually shown any interest in the tent up to this point. Then Yu Ling remembered: the developers had been keen to sell the estate as pet friendly, so every house in Golden Lake Villas was fitted with a special pet door. Theirs was at the end of the ground-floor passageway. Her sir hated pets and found the gap unsightly, so he'd hired workmen to fill it with bricks and cover the outside with a wooden board painted white, blending into the wall. Yu Ling prized the board away and removed the bricks. Now the goose had its own entryway, as long as it was willing to lower that tall neck. She understood this wasn't the main point, and the bigger question was how to allow it to leave the back garden. If it couldn't get out, once it had finished the pile of vegetables they'd left for it, it would slowly starve to death. She decided to leave the back gate, which was normally only used for large deliveries, open just a crack. If the goose was smart enough, it would find its way out once the food was gone.

Just before they left, the boy ran after the goose to say goodbye. "Hey! It doesn't matter if you have no friends. You can play by yourself."

They left three hours before their departure time, first on foot to the bus stop, then the 942 bus to the metro station, then three stops on the Number 15 line, and another seventeen on the Number 14 line. More than ever, Yu Ling understood how difficult it was to get anywhere from Golden Lake Villas without a car. Normally she had Dong to drive her in the black people carrier with the spacious interior and outstanding sound system. He was a steady driver, and when she was in the rear with Kuan Kuan playing cards, enjoying some snacks, or watching a movie, she was never worried about time, they seemed to get anywhere they needed in a flash. The windows were tinted dark brown, and through them she watched swarms of delivery riders like flying insects, filling every crevice between vehicles at red lights, one foot on the ground, anxiously tapping at their hands-free sets or holding their phones to their mouths like walkie-talkies, scanning their surroundings in their peripheral vision for empty spaces so they could inch ahead. The more nimble among them were able to position themselves right in front, zooming ahead of the traffic as soon as the lights turned green. Down the road, the cars always caught up to them before too long. Yu Ling felt a little thrill whenever the people carrier overtook a motorbike that had pushed ahead.

Before they met, Donghu had been a delivery rider. Now she wished she'd known this version of him. In her view, there was a certain purity to this job. Every moment of a delivery rider's day was completely absorbed by whatever order they were delivering. The joys and sorrows of the people in the cars around them meant nothing, and they had no need to concern themselves with whoever was in the black people carriers overtaking then falling behind them, or whatever transactions they were carrying out. But Donghu had started paying attention to them, the gleam of their black paint in the sunlight, the purr of their engines, the way they zoomed out of view, leaving tire tracks across his heart. He got his license and became a driver. From then on, he plunged into a completely different life.

Kuan Kuan had never taken the metro. When the train roared in from the dark throat of the tunnel, he hopped with excitement. They went the wrong way while changing trains and accidentally exited the station, ending up in an underground shopping mall. Yu Ling was forced to go up to the surface to figure out where they were.

"We've been here before!" cried Kuan Kuan.

Yu Ling looked up and saw a building painted maple leaf red, its conical roof topped with a golden spire, making the whole thing look like an enormous pencil. Yes, this was the children's theater.

They used to come here once or twice a month, on weekend afternoons or evenings. Perhaps Qin Wen had happened to mention to someone that Kuan Kuan enjoyed watching plays, and that person started sending them tickets every month in a white envelope. Yu Ling enjoyed the task of picking out a couple of shows for them to see, though sometimes Qin Wen would butt in and insist they had to catch a particular play, which is how they ended up watching *King Lear for Kids*. What child would care about the story of a bad-tempered old dude? Kuan Kuan started screaming that he was bored halfway through, and Yu Ling never got to find out what happened to poor Cordelia. Probably nothing good, she thought, a woman like her who didn't know how to say the right thing.

Yu Ling could describe every detail of the foyer, including the usher with the large ears who would take their tickets without a word, ripping them along the perforated line with a gentle tug on either end. If anyone asked him where to go, he would answer without hesitation, having apparently memorized the entire seating plan. The tickets cost between ¥380 and ¥1,280, a disparity that startled Yu Ling at first. Weren't they sitting in the same room, breathing the same air, watching the same show? If there were an earthquake, they would be buried under the same rubble. Later, after careful observation, she realized how different the experience actually was. The cheapest seats were at either end of a semicircle, a narrow aisle away from the front of the stage. From here you could see the actors standing by the curtains, putting on headgear and fastening their trousers as they prepared for their entrances, the border between dream and reality, making it impossible to fully immerse yourself in the show. Besides, most of the actors had their backs to you, as if they'd left you behind. The performers always faced the people right in the center, weeping and pleading in the direction of the ¥1,280 seats. People say the poor love to dream, but that isn't quite right. Dreaming is the privilege of the moneyed, and the world has all kinds of ways to protect their dreams.

She and Kuan Kuan always sat right in the middle of the orchestra seating, the rest of the audience surrounding them in perfect equilibrium. For two hours, Yu Ling felt valued, among the most important customers. She began to feel a sense of belonging, and sincerely hoped this theater would always be the most popular one. When she realized it was in fact on the decline, with shrinking audiences, her heart ached for it. Deciding it was her duty to rescue the venue, she wrote a letter detailing its most urgent shortcomings: the air-conditioning was too cold, there were footprints on the seatbacks, they ought to turn off the lights illuminating the row numbers during blackouts. She dropped this document into the suggestion box next to the ticket office, which she'd seen them checking, though she understood it might take them a while to respond.

Now here they were at the theater, but without tickets. She probably wouldn't ever see another show here. Even if she stayed in Beijing, she wouldn't be able to spend her afternoons like that. She'd never know if they'd taken her suggestions.

She oriented herself and led them to another metro entrance at the far end of the road. She still remembered how, the year she moved to Beijing, every metro ride cost two yuan no matter how many stops you went, how many times you crisscrossed the city in those underground tunnels. When you walked up the steps to the surface, your card would only have two yuan less than before. This made sense to her. No matter how convoluted their route, people were still only paying to get to one destination. No need to worry about getting the wrong line— you were new in town and it wasn't your fault you'd gotten lost, you simply had to find the right direction and set out again for where you needed to be, all for a mere two yuan. Yu Ling had thought of the low fare as a kindness the city was doing her. Those times were gone for good. By her third year here, they'd switched to distance-based fares, making you responsible for every step you took. According to Kuan Kuan's translation, the English announcement they kept making, "Watch your step," meant roughly the same thing.

15

They didn't get lost again, and arrived at the train station early enough for a quick dinner. At McDonald's, Yu Ling ordered a burger, fried chicken, and French fries. Gobbling down this usually forbidden junk food gave the boy enormous pleasure.

He held a fry between two fingers and mimed smoking before trying to stuff it into Yu Ling's mouth.

"You have that one," she said, but he just tried to feed her another one, and then another. He kept this up, blank faced, pretending to be a robot. She tickled him until he capitulated and laughed.

"Enough?" she said. Unable to stop laughing, the boy held up his hands in surrender.

"Your son is so lively," said the woman in a woolly hat at the next table. When Yu Ling looked at her askance, she hastily added, "There's nothing wrong with being lively! Lively boys are more intelligent."

"He's very annoying," Yu Ling grumbled. Although she'd been out alone with Kuan Kuan many times over the years, this was the first time she'd been mistaken for his mother. You could tell at once that Kuan Kuan was a rich kid, while she looked like a nanny. What was different about today?

"How long are we going for?" said Kuan Kuan. "If I don't like it there, can we come back right away?"

"You'll like it there."

"Do you think the swan has gone inside the house?"

"Don't you worry, it's very clever."

They went back to the departure hall and headed to their ticket gate. Yu Ling managed to find an empty seat and held Kuan Kuan on her lap. The crowd bustled around them. Someone bumped Kuan Kuan's head as they pushed past. The man next to them put a call on speaker, as if he was competing to be louder than everyone around them. Kuan Kuan glared furiously at him, but he was oblivious. When he finally hung up, the boy yelled, "Stupid pig!"

The man stared at Kuan Kuan. Yu Ling hastily apologized, grabbed the boy's hand, and walked away. As soon as they were out of sight, she began berating him. If he went around saying such things away from home, she said, he'd get beaten up.

"Away from home?" muttered the boy, then lapsed into silence.

They stood in a quiet corner until it was almost time for their train. Yu Ling took the boy to the restroom. She splashed some water on her face and went back out to wait for him. When he didn't emerge, she asked a passing man to look in the gents, but he said there were no little boys in there. Worried that the man from earlier was taking revenge, she hurried back to where they'd been, but a different person was sitting there. She sprinted to their gate. All the passengers had boarded, and there was no one around but the ticket inspectors. She asked if they'd let a child through, and they said no. She ran past all the gates, and then the McDonald's. Finally she went to Information and had them make an announcement.

"Hu Yikuan, please come to the second-floor information booth, you have family waiting for you."

All she'd said was that she wasn't the boy's mother, and they hadn't asked any more. Simpler to label her "family." Vague, but also a little heartwarming. This tenderness caused her a pang. The woman at the desk looked at her sympathetically.

"Don't worry. I almost lost my son one time, when he was little."

She checked every exit, then the metro station, asking the attendants if they'd seen a seven-year-old boy. No one had. Finally, she picked up the luggage she'd left at the information booth and dragged it out of the station.

According to the clock tower, it was nine o'clock. She had to stare at it for quite a while before making out where the hands were. Her eyes were blurring, and she felt waves of dizziness. She tried to go up the overhead bridge, thinking she could see farther from there, but her legs refused to obey her, and walked straight ahead instead. She found herself in the taxi queue.

"To the police station," she said to the driver.

"Which one?"

"The nearest one."

The driver pointed out that there were police officers in the train station, but she didn't seem to hear him, and refused to get out of the car. Ten minutes later, the driver kicked her out at a precinct a few streets away. The gold crest looked duller in the dark, but the words "Public Security" jumped out in stark white. What would she tell them? That she, a nanny, had lost her charge? Would they allow her to walk out, or would they arrest her? Perhaps they'd detain her until she'd explained the whole situation. What situation? Would that include her and Donghu taking the child on a "spring outing"? What if they thought Donghu had taken the child? No, that wasn't right, she'd have to talk about the money she'd lost, and explain why she hadn't reported that to the police. Why would they believe her? They'd probably have to bring Donghu in to corroborate her account, and until they found him, they'd keep her locked up. With a shiver, she turned and walked briskly away, stopping herself from breaking into a run for fear of attracting attention.

Even if she didn't go to the police, they would come looking for her sooner or later. There was no way she could disclaim responsibility for a missing child. She glanced at the train station clock tower and felt she ought to leave Beijing as soon as possible.

She called her mother, and was greeted by a squall of baby cries. She sat on the curb and waited for her mother to calm the child down. Her mother soothed the baby with a series of nonsense nicknames: darling, treasure, carrot, pumpkin, dumpling, bun. Like chanting spells to put him to sleep. One of them must have worked, because the child gradually quieted down.

This was her little brother's second child, the longed-for

grandson. After he was born, Yu Ling's mother sold her house and gave the money to the brother, who bought a house in the county seat. Her mother then moved in with them, to help Yu Ling's sister-in-law with childcare. Yu Ling said she might come back for a visit, but her mother immediately said there wasn't room for her in the house, and besides, her sister-in-law was always in a temper because she was having trouble breast-feeding.

Something startled the baby awake, and he resumed bawling.

"You ought to buy him a pacifier," said Yu Ling.

"No, all plastic contains poison," said her mother. "You were just here a few months ago, you want to come back again? What's wrong, are they still giving you grief over your little problem?"

"No, I'm just tired, I need a break."

"I keep telling you, you need to learn to cut corners. Don't let the kid sit around, tire him out so he goes to bed early and you'll get your time back."

"I'm not looking after the child anymore."

"What else can you do? Did your friend from jail look you up?"

"Who?"

"The scrawny monkey—you were always going for a smoke with her. Wasn't she trying to get you to sell health supple-ments?"

"That was ages ago! I lost touch with her."

"Those supplements were poison. You'd die if you took them."

Yu Ling felt her mother's understanding of her had frozen at some point in the past. Probably when she went to prison. That's when her mother lost hope and placed all her aspirations on her brother instead. There were times where her brother or sister-in-law treated her mother badly, and she would phone Yu Ling in tears to complain—but if Yu Ling dared to criticize her brother in any way, her mother would jump to his defense immediately.

"You have no idea how much your brother and I suffered before your father died," her mother always said, as if this explained everything.

Yu Ling ended the call and stood up. She wouldn't be going back to Gansu Province, then. Of course, she could go literally anywhere else, just get a train to a random city, walk out of the station, and melt into the crowd. Whenever she left somewhere, she cut herself off cold turkey from everyone she'd known in that place, because she would never go back. Where could Kuan Kuan have run off to? Had a human trafficker nabbed him? Was he waiting for her to rescue him? She'd allowed him to end up in danger—how could she abandon him now? But maybe he'd simply wandered off, in which case some Good Samaritan might have brought him home. She decided to return to Golden Lake Villas. If there was still no news by the following morning, she'd steel herself to go to the police.

She got another taxi back and got out at the gate. Lu, the security guard, stopped her to ask what she'd been thinking, letting the child take a taxi back alone. She froze for a second, then ran to the house as quickly as she could while pulling the suitcase. Lu yelled after her that he'd had to pay the boy's fare, she owed him! She sprinted through the dark, took a couple of deep breaths when she reached the house, and pushed the door open. Every single light in the place was on. She marched up to the tent and found the boy curled up inside, sound asleep.

She gave him a shove. "How could you do that?"

He stared at her, then snuggled into her arms. "Being away from home made me scared. I want to stay here. I don't want to go anywhere."

She felt his heartbeat, a familiar sensation. Those nights he'd squeezed into her narrow bed, she'd heard it in the dark, each throb followed closely by one of her own, call and response.

16

When she asked how he'd actually got home, Kuan Kuan answered breezily: he followed the crowd to the taxi queue, told a driver the address, and said his family would pay. But how did he get through the front door? No problem at all, he'd memorized the code.

"I bet you think you're pretty clever," said Yu Ling. "What if I hadn't come back, huh? Where do you think you'd be then?"

"I knew you'd come back."

"Why?"

"They're all gone. You have to look after the place."

"No, I don't." She looked at him. "Kuan Kuan, this isn't my home."

He sat up straight, waving his arms to take in their surroundings. "I meant this place. Swan Home is our home! Did you forget?"

That night, Yu Ling slept in the tent too. The weather was so warm they opened the windows to let in the smell of leaves.

She woke up in the middle of the night and heard the strong wind whooshing, making her feel as if the house had vanished, leaving them lying in a wilderness with just the tent to shield them.

The next morning, as soon as the boy opened his eyes, he said he wasn't going to Nanning, and if she insisted on taking him, he'd run away again. Yu Ling phoned Guangxi and said the boy refused to travel, could they send someone to Beijing to look after him?

"We can't go to Beijing. Why won't you understand that? We can't go anywhere!" The woman was getting worked up. "It's this damn investigation! As long as it's going on, we won't have a single day's peace." She burst into tears, her sobbing much higher than her raspy voice, as if she'd been startled awake from a dream. The weeping cut off abruptly; probably she'd put down the phone. When she came back, she sounded calm again.

"Take care of the boy for now. We can talk again when things have quieted down."

Before ending the call, Yu Ling asked the woman a question that had been on her mind for some time: Who was she? Kuan Kuan's aunt, perhaps?

"I'm nothing at all," said the woman, and hung up.

That afternoon, Yu Ling cleaned the house from top to bottom, disposing of the shriveled lilies in the vases and changing

Kuan Kuan's sheets. Through the second-floor window, she watched Kuan Kuan chase the goose around the yard, trying to train it to use the pet door. The goose didn't seem to have done any exploring while they were gone, neither entering the house nor trying to leave the garden. Of course, it hadn't finished the food they'd left for it. The boy had another plan; with a bamboo pole, he placed a line of cabbage leaves down the tunnel, hoping the goose would follow the trail to the other side. Alas, the goose wasn't hungry and only nibbled at the cabbage before waddling away. The boy ran after it.

Yu Ling went back to work. By the time she was done, she'd worked up quite a sweat and needed a shower. She realized she was out of shower gel and went to get some from her ma'am's bathroom. Faced with a shelf of colorful bottles, she sniffed at them one by one. Some were so lushly fragranced they made her dizzy. After a few minutes, she found herself filling the bathtub and slipping in. The sides of the tub were so cool and smooth, like a lady's skin, she felt a little embarrassed to lean back against it. She pressed the buttons for the massage jets. Columns of water spurted out, now hitting her back, now her legs. She hesitated between several types of soap, unsure which would produce the most bubbles. Finally she selected one, but even after she'd lathered it for ages, it only produced a thin slick of foam. She sank down, resting her head on the lip of the tub, just the way Qin Wen did.

Where was Qin Wen at this moment? Hong Kong was part of China, so she wouldn't be able to go anywhere she had to show her papers. Yu Ling thought of the fishing village in Sai Kung where the family had had a seafood meal. The fishy-smelling restaurants, the wetness at each entrance. She imagined a windowless room in one of those low buildings, and Qin Wen sitting on the edge of a single bed, staring blankly in the gloom.

That makes you happy, doesn't it? she heard Duomei say. That wasn't fair. It wasn't as if she'd been hoping for Qin Wen's downfall all along. She didn't want anything bad to happen to her. Sure, she'd tried to kidnap her son, but that was completely different. Yu Ling thought of her actions as a necessary response, to make Qin Wen understand she wouldn't be so easily bullied. Anyway, the way she'd planned it, the child would have been unharmed, and Qin Wen would only have lost a bit of cash. Duomei had said many people loathed her, as if hatred was a righteous thing, as if you could hate with abandon. Yu Ling didn't loathe Qin Wen. To be accurate, she was merely disappointed in her.

The incident took place last August. The whole family was due to spend Christmas in the States, and Qin Wen abruptly asked Yu Ling if she'd like to come along. Yu Ling hadn't thought too much about it, she just assumed Kuan Kuan needed her, that he'd be on edge without her there, so she agreed. Then she was denied a visa. Afterward, she often thought back to that afternoon in the American consulate, the way the golden-haired man at the counter looked her up and down without a word. Perhaps his disdain was concealed by his full beard, and she was lulled into thinking he might be friendly. Soon, she learned of the rejection. *They picked you out*, Hui had said, *like a rotten apple from the barrel.*

The atmosphere changed after that. While the family was

away, Qin Wen didn't ask Yu Ling to take care of the house, but gave the task to Hui instead. The work crew her sir had brought in to do repairs only took orders from Hui. Two weeks in the States, and Kuan Kuan didn't call her once. She didn't even know their return date had changed until Hui told her. Hui was strutting around, cock of the walk.

Soon after the family returned, Hui came knocking at Yu Ling's door late one night.

"So, I hear you've done time?" Hui's eyes gleamed. "What did you do?"

Yu Ling walked over and slapped her. "I killed someone. Satisfied?" She pulled the door open. "Get out."

The next morning, Hui was waiting uneasily outside her room to explain that she'd overheard Qin Wen on the phone asking someone to look into Yu Ling's background. That afternoon, Yu Ling's mother called. Apparently the village headman had sent someone over to ask some questions about the family.

"I told him the truth," said her mother in a low voice.

That night, Yu Ling handed in her notice. She didn't give a reason, she only said she was no longer interested in childcare and would only pick up hourly housework from now on. Qin Wen sat in the red velvet armchair of her workspace, flipping through the auction catalog in her lap. She didn't look up till Yu Ling was done speaking.

"It was such a long time ago, I can understand why you didn't want to bring it up. Still, it was wrong of you to hide something this important. I hope you see that."

"I'm sorry I kept this from you, I didn't mean anything bad

by it." In a surge of emotion, she blurted out, "I didn't do it. Do you believe me?"

"They must have had their reasons for sending you to jail."

Yu Ling nodded and reached into her pocket for her key card, which she left on the table as she walked out.

Qin Wen called her name. "You think you can just go back to the agency and find another job? When they know you have a record, do you think they'll keep you on their books? It will be the same if you try to find another agency." She looked Yu Ling straight in the eyes, a smile playing across her face. "I'm the only one who'll take you in now, understand? I didn't say I was firing you, which means you should keep working here."

That night, Yu Ling was back in her little room. Lying in bed, listening to the footsteps in the corridor outside, everything felt different. She'd always believed she'd chosen to work for this household, that she'd chosen to give her affection to Kuan Kuan. She was full of passion for her work, because she thought it was what she'd chosen. Now she realized she was trapped, a pathetic person who needed to be taken in. She ought to be grateful, to work uncomplainingly for her employers, until the day they no longer needed her, whereupon she would leave this place like an obsolete appliance. She was sad for a few days, and when she saw Kuan Kuan, he looked strange to her. As if Qin Wen's features could faintly be glimpsed beneath the child's innocent face. With time, the sorrow transformed into rage. A small joke from Kuan Kuan was enough to propel her into a temper. That was when Donghu once again mentioned his scheme, more seriously this time.

The door slammed open: Kuan Kuan. Yu Ling hastily submerged herself.

"Get out!" she yelled. How embarrassing, to be caught lounging in his mother's tub.

"You had a phone call. I told him to call back later."

"You answered?"

"I talked to him for a while." Kuan Kuan shrugged and left.

It was Dalei. He'd tried to get Kuan Kuan to say where Donghu was, but when the boy realized what he wanted, he put on a grown-up voice and said the information was worth five thousand yuan. When Dalei phoned again, he told Yu Ling he no longer cared about tracking Donghu down and just wanted to sort out the trouble he'd caused.

"I spoke to the guy who lent me the van, and he said I need to pay him back thirty grand," said Dalei. "You're Donghu's girlfriend, you could at least help me out with that."

"Why would you help Donghu borrow a van?" grumbled Yu Ling. "It was greed, wasn't it? You thought you'd get a share of the money. And now you've made a loss instead, you don't want to pay up?"

"Calm down, I didn't say I won't pay. I was just asking if you could chip in."

"Oh, sure, I'll send you everything I have in my account." Yu Ling laughed grimly.

She told Dalei about Donghu making off with all her savings, though not a word about the spring outing, which probably made her sound like a silly lovesick girl who'd been willingly duped. When she was done, Dalei gently scolded her, "You women are always getting taken in by men's looks. You ought to have known right away that someone like him couldn't be trusted." He was silent a moment, then asked Yu Ling if she was struggling, if she needed to borrow some money. This sudden gesture of kindness embarrassed her. She realized that she was almost like a swindler too.

17

Kuan Kuan's prediction from a few days ago came true: he had a fever. Maybe he'd gotten overtired from the trip to the train station or caught a chill from sleeping in the tent. In any case, it was down to Yu Ling's negligence, ruining her record—at this point, she'd managed to keep the boy from getting sick for a full two years.

She gave him some pills, but his temperature remained high. He kept tossing and turning, only managing short bursts of sleep. He said he'd dreamed of the white cat they'd found in the forest. This was the third time, he confessed. Bugs were eating its eyes. Worst of all, it told Kuan Kuan there was so much dirt pressing down on it, it couldn't even roll over. Yu Ling told him the cat wouldn't feel the weight once it fell asleep. The boy asked what if it couldn't sleep, what if it was just stuck underground, eyes wide open? Yu Ling said no, it would sleep, it needed a good rest.

"Just remember that it means well, it's not going to hurt you," said Yu Ling.

"Yes. I'm not scared of it."

The boy leaned against her, kneading her earlobes till he dropped off.

An hour later, he stirred awake. "Has Grandpa finished his meeting yet?"

No, said Yu Ling. She thought for a moment before adding that actually she wasn't sure, maybe he was done and had gone back to Yunnan.

The boy shook his head. "He'd definitely have come to see me. He told me he only has meetings in Beijing so he can visit me." He rolled over to face the ceiling. "Does Mama know I'm sick?"

Yu Ling said yes.

"And Baba? Why haven't they phoned me yet?"

Yu Ling said they still had stuff to do, and the boy stopped asking questions. Eventually, Yu Ling broke the silence: "How could you ask for money on the phone? Who taught you to do that?"

"I wanted to buy the rest of the swans," said the boy weakly. He drifted off again, his breathing growing deep, but his brow was still furrowed.

Yu Ling took his temperature again: 39.8°C. She decided to go downstairs for some ice to cool him down.

The ice cube tray was frozen solid, and she had to bash it hard against the side of the sink, which made such a racket she didn't hear the doorbell. Only when she stopped did she realize it must have been ringing for some time. The quick, repeated bursts of buzzing indicated that the visitor was rapidly losing patience.

Yu Ling opened the door to find a woman in a flowery dress, face thickly caked in powder, her bright lipstick so lavishly applied it had spilled over onto her philtrum. She was easily five foot eleven, eclipsing Yu Ling in her shadow.

"I was starting to think no one was home." The giantess pushed Yu Ling aside with her sturdy arm and strode into the living room.

She placed herself in the center of the couch, which was too low for her, forcing her to splay her legs open. When she noticed Yu Ling staring, she adjusted her skirt and daintily cleared her throat.

"This is Hu Yafei's home, isn't it?"

Yu Ling said he was out.

"I know, they took him away." She gave Yu Ling a sweeping glance. "You must be the nanny. Where's the child?"

"Asleep."

"Pour me a glass of water. The hot pot was too spicy tonight." She fanned herself, as if this might cool down her throat.

"And who might you be?"

"Me?" The woman batted her eyelids. "My name is Huang Xiaomin, I'm Hu Yafei's girlfriend." She shrugged in the face of Yu Ling's surprise. "What's the big deal?" She rose to her feet and walked around the room, glancing up at the chandelier dangling from the double-height ceiling. "Ever since I was a little girl, I've been afraid of walking into light fixtures. All ceilings ought to be this high, don't you think?"

Yu Ling went to the kitchen to get the water, and Huang

Xiaomin followed her to the doorway. "Is that ice? Let me have some." Out of restlessness or boredom, she began jumping to tap the top of the doorframe. Yu Ling handed her the iced water and she guzzled it, her broad nostrils flaring in a way that reminded Yu Ling of a horse.

"Can I help you?" said Yu Ling. "I need to get back to the child, he has a fever."

Xiaomin put down her glass. "Kuan Kuan's ill? Where is he?" She galloped up the stairs. When Yu Ling followed with a bag of ice and basin of water, she saw the woman popping something in the boy's mouth. Yu Ling ran over and grabbed his face.

"What did you give him?"

"A mint."

"Spit it out, Kuan Kuan."

The boy, now fully awake, pursed his lips. "It's sweet."

"Yes, it is," said Xiaomin. "It's from the hot pot restaurant. It will cool you down."

Yu Ling glared at her before lifting Kuan Kuan into a sitting position and unbuttoning his pajama top to give him a sponge bath. Xiaomin pulled over a chair and sat in front of the boy. "I'm your baba's girlfriend. He often mentions you. Apparently you're a great piano player."

"I hate practicing," said the boy indistinctly.

"I hated it too," said Xiaomin. "My ma forced me to practice every day, until I threw my instrument into the toilet."

"Whoa! How did you do that?"

Xiaomin held up a hand and flexed her strong fingers. "Oh,

it was just an electronic keyboard. An expensive one, though. Yamaha."

"Could you move a little?" said Yu Ling, turning to her.

Xiaomin shifted her chair backward. "Remember when your baba came back from Hong Kong with a toy airplane for you? I helped him choose the model."

"Ma won't let me play with it, she's afraid I'll smash her vases." Kuan Kuan lifted his arms so Yu Ling could clean his armpits.

Xiaomin sighed. "They're only vases."

"Where's the plane?" Kuan Kuan asked Yu Ling. She pushed him back down and put the ice pack on his forehead. Go to sleep, she said, he could play when he felt better.

Xiaomin squeezed his palm. "Poor little mite. Sleep well." The boy shifted uneasily and moaned a little before shutting his eyes.

Xiaomin followed Yu Ling back into the kitchen, and watched as she washed some rice. "Is that your dinner? Add a bit more rice, would you? I'd like some congee too." She opened the fridge door, studied its contents, and grabbed a can of soda water. As she drank, she kicked off her leather shoes and began flexing her feet. Her nude stockings made her legs look huge, the calves bulging with muscle. Her arms were strapping too, and the scarlet polish on her nails made Yu Ling think of the finger-shaped cookies Kuan Kuan had brought home from school last Halloween. Yu Ling didn't understand her sir's taste. He was a skinny man, not particularly tall. She pictured him next to this woman. Quite an odd couple. Then again, he was always going to the gym, presumably to bulk up. Maybe it was aspirational, choosing a larger woman.

"Why are you here?" said Yu Ling.

"What's going to happen to the child?"

"He's going to stay with his grandmother. Someone's coming for him later."

Xiaomin narrowed her eyes. "What does that mean, 'later'?"

"What do you have in mind?"

"I'm his girlfriend. Now something's happened to him, I can't just stand by."

Yu Ling served the congee with a dish of pickled vegetables and a slab of fermented tofu. Xiaomin sat across the table and helped herself to most of the tofu.

"Don't you have any questions for me?"

"Such as?"

"Don't you want to know about me and Yafei? I thought nannies love gossip."

"The other nanny did, but you're too late—she's gone now."

"But you stayed? Why?"

"You think I should have left the child to fend for himself?"

"Of course not. You're being very helpful. I'll make sure I tell Yafei when I see him."

"No need. I'll leave when the boy's grandma sends someone for him."

"Now, what was I going to say?" Xiaomin frowned in thought. "Oh yes, Yafei and I are moving in together. He's planning to divorce Qin Wen. If only he'd done it sooner, he wouldn't have been taken away."

"What about Kuan Kuan?"

"He'll come with us, of course," said Xiaomin staunchly. "Qin Wen doesn't like kids. I'll be good to him. I've told Yafei we don't need another child."

"What are your plans?"

"I'll wait for him. I've asked around, and his charges aren't too serious. He should be out in three to five years. I'll visit him in the meantime. Bring him nice things to eat."

"You can't bring food on prison visits."

Xiaomin pouted. "Fine, I'll knit him sweaters."

"What about Qin Wen? Will they find her?"

"I thought you didn't like gossip? Why, did you get on well with her?"

"I need to check on Kuan Kuan." Yu Ling stood up.

"I'll come with you."

18

The boy had said he wanted to see the moon, so the bedroom curtains remained open. Through the window glass, the almond-yellow crescent looked embalmed in pine resin. The boy slept with his mouth wide open, breathing laboriously. Yu Ling took his temperature again: still over 39. She rubbed him down with a damp cloth. Xiaomin asked why she wasn't giving him medicine.

"Haven't you ever had a fever? You can only take these pills once every four hours."

"No, I've never been ill."

Yu Ling changed the ice pack and glanced at the clock on the bedside table. Still an hour till his next dose. She sat by his bed to wait. Xiaomin went back downstairs and returned with a cookie jar. She settled on the floor by the window lamp and carefully read the label.

"Thirty-one grams of fat!" With a sigh, she reached in anyway.

"Good for you, being able to eat at a time like this."

"Life is full of uncertainty. I only pay attention to the things I can be sure of." Xiaomin dusted cookie crumbs off her hands.

Yu Ling gave Kuan Kuan a fever pill, followed by a large glass of water. He lay back down but kept writhing, kicking the covers off. Yu Ling had to hold down the blanket in one hand, the ice pack in the other. The boy slowly settled. She turned to Xiaomin and found her asleep on the carpet, head pillowed on a crocodile plushie, legs flung over the armrest of a kiddie chair, half-open mouth letting out low hoots as if she had a whistle in there.

Yu Ling leaned back, her drowsiness completely gone. She didn't understand Hu Yafei at all. Of course, it would have been a surprise to find out that Huang Xiaomin was anyone's girlfriend. But also, it had never crossed her mind that her sir might have a lover. He'd always seemed so proper, and treated Qin Wen well. Qin Wen was the more unstable one of the couple. She often fell into bad moods that involved her screaming at her husband, claiming it was his fault she couldn't be an artist. Hu Yafei never argued back, just sat quietly and waited for her to regain her senses.

"It's okay, everything's fine," he would say, rubbing the back of Qin Wen's neck as if she were a little cat. Now Yu Ling thought about it, there was something lofty in his tenderness. He never lost his dignity, because everything was perpetually under his control. He decided everything about this household. Even his silence had something strategic about it. Yu Ling was always slightly afraid of him, but maybe that was her problem. Ever since she was a child, she'd feared men with authority: her father, the village headman, the school principal, the factory foreman. Speaking to them, she'd feel herself tense up, uncertain what orders they would give. No matter what they said, she'd find herself unable to refuse. Hence she avoided meeting their gaze, as if that would prevent them from noticing her. Over the last four years, she and Hu Yafei had barely made eye contact, which kept her feeling safe.

Not that Yu Ling believed everything Huang Xiaomin was telling her. At the very least, it seemed unlikely Hu Yafei had been planning to divorce Qin Wen. Without the backing of his father-in-law, his business wouldn't have been able to carry on, leaving him no different from any ordinary person. Yu Ling was surprised at herself, only realizing this now. Before this, she'd never stopped to consider what actually gave these men their authority. They seemed to simply appear in these positions, occupying them as a matter of course. Perhaps right now, Hu Yafei wished he were an ordinary person. If Xiaomin was right and he'd be out of prison in three to five years, would he divorce Qin Wen and take Kuan Kuan away from her? That would leave Qin Wen with nothing at all.

Art always begins with loss. Yu Ling recalled Qin Wen saying these words, the expression on her face something like envy.

Xiaomin slept till almost noon. She ran downstairs, makeup smeared, mascara clumped beneath her eyes.

"Where's Kuan Kuan? How is he?"

"I'm here," Kuan Kuan piped up, sitting wanly at the table stirring his oatmeal.

Xiaomin patted his head. "Remember me? Your baba's girlfriend."

"I remember. You said you were going to play airplane with me."

"And then some. I know all kinds of games. I used to run a fat camp. As soon as they woke up we'd start playing, and we wouldn't stop till bedtime. They loved me to death. They cried and hugged me when it was time to say goodbye. Can you imagine? Cuddling a dozen little cherubs at once, it was like being surrounded by space heaters." Her actual job, she added, was a certified nutritionist. She sat down. "Anyway, let Auntie Xiaomin see to her own nutrition. I'm starving."

Yu Ling served her a bowl of congee, and she yelped, "Congee again? The fridge is full of delicious things, why don't you make something else?"

"Feel free to do it yourself. My job description doesn't include cooking for the kid's father's girlfriend. In fact, do me a favor and go pick up some pastries. I'll give you the address."

"Why can't you do it? You're the nanny!"

Yu Ling said nothing. Xiaomin scrambled for another excuse, claiming her shoes had given her a huge blister, whereupon Yu Ling fetched her a pair of her sir's sneakers, size 42, just right for her. Yu Ling gave her a shopping list: vegetables, meat, flour, yeast. Xiaomin protested again when Yu Ling said she'd have to use her own money, but Yu Ling said this was nothing, she'd also have to pay Kuan Kuan's school fees. Xiaomin went off in a sulk, after putting in a request: Anything but congee for dinner, please.

She returned at three in the afternoon with all the items on Yu Ling's list, plus a suitcase. Given the circumstances, she said, she was prepared to look after the child long-term. She didn't really know how to cook or do any housework, but Yu Ling could teach her, she was a fast learner. She lugged the suitcase up the stairs and attempted to bring it into the main bedroom, but Yu Ling blocked her way.

"No one's using it," Xiaomin protested.

"Then let it stay empty."

"I suppose you want to move in yourself."

"I said, let it stay empty."

Yu Ling settled Xiaomin in the second-story guest room. Kuan Kuan woke a short time later and perked up after having a couple of pastries. He ran around looking for his swan, and snuck outside while Yu Ling was busy making dinner. Almost right away, he forgot he wasn't supposed to be there, and yelled for them to come see. Yu Ling and Xiaomin ran out to find the goose by the side of the pond. It picked up a piece of bread in its beak and tossed it into the water. The koi, already teeming, swarmed into a tighter knot. Two of the more anxious ones leaped from the water.

The goose straightened its neck, swiveled its head, and reached for more bread.

"It's feeding the fish?" whispered Xiaomin.

"Where did the bread come from?" Yu Ling asked.

"I bought it while I was out. I put half the loaf aside in case you tried to feed me congee again."

"It can help with our chores!" said Kuan Kuan, clapping his hands.

"This is nothing compared to the damage it's caused," grumbled Yu Ling. "It keeps pecking at the flowerpots and scattering soil everywhere."

"Geese have really unusual eyesight," said Xiaomin. "Everything looks smaller to them than it really is."

"How do you know?" said the boy.

"My family used to rear geese."

"This is a swan."

"Don't argue with him," said Yu Ling. "He believes it can fly."

"Do you know why a goose attacks people?" said Xiaomin. "Because in its eyes, it's bigger than a human being."

"Does it think it's bigger than a horse?" asked the boy.

"It thinks it's bigger than everything."

"It must think it's the king of the forest!"

"It doesn't care about being king, but it isn't scared of anything."

Hearing movement, the goose swung around abruptly and stood its ground, staring unblinkingly at them.

Kuan Kuan took a couple of steps forward, waving. "Hello! Welcome to Lilliput!"

19

Dinner was sweet-and-sour pork, shrimp and cashew stir-fry, steamed grouper with fermented soybeans, and braised spinach. Kuan Kuan preferred Cantonese-style sweet-and-sour pork, but Yu Ling had forgotten to put pineapple on the shopping list. Xiaomin praised Yu Ling's cooking skills extravagantly. Yu Ling could open a restaurant, she said. There was something infectious about the way Xiaomin enjoyed her food—her enthusiasm made everything seem extra delicious, and you ate more than you meant to. For once, Kuan Kuan wasn't picky. He even tussled with Xiaomin for the last piece of pork.

Later that evening, after Kuan Kuan had gone to bed, Yu Ling decided to bake some bread. Xiaomin offered to help, but after she got eggshell fragments in the dough and spilled flour everywhere, Yu Ling banned her from touching anything. The most annoying thing about Xiaomin was the noise she produced when she so much as moved a plate. Yu Ling felt the whole point of having a state-of-the-art kitchen was that it operated in silence. Even when the oven, microwave, blender, extractor fan, dishwasher, and mixer were all going, you shouldn't hear much. Just a low hum at most, the appliances drawing breath. Sometimes at bedtime, Kuan Kuan would suddenly demand a particular cake or bread for the next day, and although Yu Ling would grumble, she'd actually be delighted. She was free to use the kitchen anytime, but it felt safer to have an unimpeachable reason that would allow her to linger.

Best of all was working here in the middle of the night. With everything quiet, she could hear the wind rustling through the bamboo grove by the window, casting shadows that ebbed and flowed like tides. The cakes she made were usually quite simple, it was just a question of mixing various ingredients together, all of them equally important—unlike bread, where every batch of dough had its own personality, just like people. Some stubborn, some gentle, some mischievous. Yu Ling only had to sink her fingers into a batch to know what kind of dough she was dealing with.

That night, she was making cranberry walnut bread. After kneading the dough, she gently lifted it off the mat and into a ceramic bowl. There was astounding potential in it now. With heat, countless air pockets would open up within it, doubling or trebling its size. Sometimes she enjoyed watching for it to burst its skin. One of her many little superstitions: witnessing this moment brought good fortune.

The village she came from farmed wheat. She'd always enjoyed playing with dough, and had known from a young age that yeast made for softer steamed buns. They were too stingy with their yeast, though, and never allowed the dough to ex-pand enough to rip its own surface, as if that would transform it into something else. If her grandmother could see the bread she was making now, she'd definitely think Yu Ling was ruin-ing these grains. Of course, there was no way they could have made bread back then, no matter how much yeast they used— they didn't have an oven.

She put the mixing bowl into the proofing drawer. She'd only turned it on a few minutes ago, but it was already at tem-perature. Such impressive speed and accuracy.

"I love their gas range. Sometimes I feel as if I'm working for it," the woman from Yu Ling's hometown had said, the one who introduced her to the agency when she first arrived in Bei-jing. Likewise, there were moments when Yu Ling felt her real employer was this oven. She was sad whenever she thought she might not see it again. The day before the "spring outing," she made a loaf of bread as a farewell. When she was done, she'd polished the oven to a shine, inside and out.

She'd met Donghu when he was working as a chauffeur for one of Hu Yafei's friends, driving a BMW 7 Series. He loved saying to Yu Ling that he'd buy the same car himself one of these days. Yu Ling had heard talk like that from other nan-nies. When they got together, their favorite game was "If I could only take one thing from the house I work at." Dish-washers, strollers, massage chairs . . . They swore they would someday buy one exactly the same, though these dreams would never be realized. The fact that they couldn't afford these things was just one reason. Even if they had the cash, these objects wouldn't fit into their lives at all. They'd sit there awkwardly, unable to function as designed. Just imagine if, someday in the future, she were to buy a small house in her hometown of Li county, Longnan city. Would she want an oven like this one? Even if she somehow had thick enough walls that an oven could be installed in them, would she still feel like baking bread in the middle of the night? Once a person's circumstances change, her happiness changes too. She understood the technological capabilities of this house, but that knowledge wouldn't help her in the future, and in fact would only add to her torment. That's why being a nanny or chauffeur is such a cruel job. You get immersed in a different way of life, molding you into a particular shape, but this only makes you look ridiculous when you're back to your own existence, like a wall-mounted oven stranded outdoors. So you need to change yourself back to the way you were before, to return to your original life. But is this even possible?

Then again, what do rich people get out of it? They might have fancy appliances, but you'll never find their fingerprints on a single "on" switch. They have no idea that the miracle of these machines isn't that the food they produce is more delicious—it's human beings making the food, after all—but the joy they provide to the people operating them. When a machine anticipates your needs, eliciting a knowing smile from you, you feel the world exists for your sake. Yu Ling remembered Donghu telling her that when he first started working as a chauffeur, he felt something like lovesickness, lying awake all night longing for dawn so he could see the car again. He enjoyed pausing briefly as he put the key in the ignition, relishing

the utter silence as if the entire world were motionless in antic-
ipation, before the dashboard lit up and the car roared to life
like waking from a dream. He always tried to reach his destination as quickly as possible so he could be alone with the car
after dropping off his sir, free to fiddle with the controls as
much as he liked. He thought there were probably functions he
wasn't aware of, so when he had time he would drive to the 4S
dealership and ask the VIP after-care staff to talk him through
what else the car could do. Finally, one of the salespeople said
to him, "You know so much you could probably come and
work here." Donghu was livid—up till then, he'd thought they
wouldn't be able to tell he was a chauffeur. But what else could
he be? What sort of tycoon would spend so much time hanging
out at a dealership?

Oh, Donghu, she thought. *Forget the BMW, just use the
money to lead a good life.*

She and Xiaomin sat at the white marble counter. The glow
of the oven reminded Yu Ling of the egg incubators they'd had
when she was a little girl. She topped up their mugs from the
electric kettle. The tea bags bobbed in the water, releasing a
faint lavender scent.

"Did you say Kuan Kuan's American?" said Yu Ling.

"Yup. He was born in the States, wasn't he?"

"Does that mean he'll have to go back to America when he's
grown up? What if he doesn't like it there?"

"Why wouldn't he like it there? Everyone there is free. No
one looks down on anyone else. They're all so friendly, they
wave hello as soon as they see you."

"You've been?"

"Yes, but not for years, maybe it's changed." Xiaomin lowered her gaze and was silent for a moment. "When Yafei gets out, we'll go live there with Kuan Kuan."

"Shouldn't the child stay with his mother?" said Yu Ling uncertainly.

"Where's his mother, then?" Xiaomin stood up, stretched, and went to study the contents of the fridge. "How far in advance did they pay your wages?" She picked up a jar of honey for a closer look.

"Why? Are you going to take over the payments?"

Xiaomin smiled. "I wish I could. You cook so well, whoever lives with you is lucky. But I'm going to be looking after the kid, so I won't be able to work. Where would I get the money to pay you? I'm not going to keep you here, you should just go. Don't worry—I'll take good care of the boy."

"I might not say yes if you tried to hire me, but you definitely don't have the power to fire me. Kuan Kuan's mother gave me this job, and I need to hear it from her if I'm leaving." Yu Ling realized she was borrowing Miss Amy's tone. It felt good.

"You're so weird. You were the one who said you'd been planning to leave." Xiaomin shut the fridge and left the kitchen.

Yu Ling added more hot water to her mug and turned to look at the oven. In the soft glow of the interior light, the bread was rising imperceptibly. For a split second, it looked to her like a vast golden seed, ready to crack open and sprout.

20

Kuan Kuan slept till noon the next day. He was in high spirits when he woke up, completely well again. He jumped out of bed and went to find Xiaomin. She was in the basement rec room playing on the dance mat. She asked him to join her, but he said no, he wanted to play with his plane. Xiaomin got it from Yu Ling, put in some batteries, and handed it to him.

With the remote control in his hands, Kuan Kuan took aim at a vase on the side table, but the airplane refused to obey instructions and looped back at them instead. The boy tried a few times, now higher, now lower, but the plane would only go in circles. Finally, Xiaomin picked it up and lobbed it at the vase. It arced through the air and nose-dived into its target. The vase wobbled and smashed to the ground, shattering into fragments.

"Yay! That one next!" Kuan Kuan pointed to the vase on the other side of the table.

Xiaomin took the plane, retreated a few meters, and let it

rip. It zoomed straight at the neck of the vase. Another crash. Kuan Kuan cheered and said they should do the folding screen next, but Yu Ling stepped in. "Go play outside," she said sternly to Xiaomin.

They were nowhere to be seen when she'd finished making dinner, so she went out into the yard. Xiaomin was twisting Kuan Kuan's arm and pushing him to the ground.

"What are you doing?" she yelled.

"And that's called an elbow hold. Got it?" Xiaomin released the boy.

"Again!" he cried. Xiaomin bent down and allowed him to grab hold of her collar. They stared at each other, unmoving, until Xiaomin's arms shot out to grab his hand and elbow. With a twist, she pressed down on his arm, forcing him to his knees.

"That's enough for today." She released him, stood with her legs together, and bowed. He returned the salute.

"If you want me to take you on as a disciple, you'll have to stop being so picky. Eat everything on your plate, especially the vegetables. Also, stretch and come jogging with me in the mornings."

"Sure!" Kuan Kuan smacked his chest.

"He has a natural talent for tae kwon do," said Xiaomin to Yu Ling as they walked back into the house.

"You'll have to talk to his father about that. He wants the boy to play baseball."

"What, just standing there with a wooden bat? That sounds like the most boring thing in the world. He'll have to take my lead when it comes to fitness."

At dinner, Kuan Kuan insisted that Xiaomin take his mother's chair. His appetite was good, and he kept asking Yu Ling for more rice.

"Can Auntie Xiaomin sleep in Swan Home with me tonight?" he asked.

"Don't ask me, just do as you like," said Yu Ling.

"See! I knew she would say yes." He winked at Xiaomin.

"But she looks angry." She winked back.

"Why would I be angry? As long as he eats his food and doesn't get sick, I don't care about anything else."

Before bedtime, Yu Ling handed Xiaomin a pillow, and reminded her to make sure Kuan Kuan didn't kick the covers off, or he might catch a chill. As she closed the tent flap, she heard Xiaomin screaming, "Let go of me or I'll give you a roundhouse kick!"

Heading to the stairs, Yu Ling spotted the goose sitting by the piano stool, the jet-black piano making it look even whiter. She'd seen it in the yard earlier that evening, and no one had opened the door since. Had it come in through the tunnel? Perhaps it was sleeping in here because the weather was too cold outside.

"You seem quite clever." She looked at it, and it stared back with its inky eyes.

There was something small and green in front of it. She tiptoed over to see what it was, but the goose immediately reared up, though at least it didn't spread its wings or make any noise. Very good, thought Yu Ling. I might appear small to you, but that doesn't mean you can attack me. She took a couple of steps forward and the goose retreated a pace, then was motionless again. Now she could see the object clearly: a Lego brick.

"You found yourself a toy?" Yu Ling bent down to pick it up, but the goose flapped its wings and honked at her. She pulled her hand back and went over to the wall to turn off the living room lights. She looked back when she got to the staircase, and the goose was once again sitting down, the Lego brick before it like a jade-green leaf.

Back in her room, Yu Ling lay in bed but couldn't sleep. After a while, there was a knock at the door and Xiaomin stuck her head in.

"Kuan Kuan keeps pinching my ear. Also, the tent is so small I can't stretch out my legs. He's asleep now. Can I go back to my bed?"

"You don't need my permission."

Xiaomin pushed open the door and leaned against the frame, rotating her wrists. "You don't actually want to leave, do you?" She glanced at Yu Ling and lowered her arms. "I don't understand. Do you plan to stay here till you die? Don't you want a life of your own?"

"Please get out, I'm trying to sleep." Yu Ling rolled over to face the wall.

21

The next morning, after Yu Ling finished making break-fast, she noticed that neither Xiaomin nor Kuan Kuan was in the living room. An engine roared outside. When she flung open the door, her sir's sports car was parked there, windows down. From the driver's seat, Xiaomin said, "I'm taking Kuan Kuan for a drive. We're going to get ice cream." She looked down to examine the controls.

"Do you have a license?"

"I got one a while back, but I don't really drive."

"No, then." Yu Ling went to the other side of the car and pulled open the door. "Out you come, Kuan Kuan."

"No! I haven't had a car ride for so long!"

"You shouldn't be in this car. There isn't even a car seat."

"There wasn't one in Uncle Melon's van either."

"Get out, Kuan Kuan! Do you hear me?" When the boy stayed put, Yu Ling reached past Xiaomin to grab the keys.

"Hey! What are you doing?" Xiaomin got out of the car.

"Give us back the keys!" Kuan Kuan jumped out too, screaming.

She'd already marched up the steps to the front door.

"Driving is easy," said Xiaomin. "You only think it's hard because you can't drive."

"Yes, she can," said Kuan Kuan.

"What did you say?" Yu Ling gaped at him.

"But she's very bad," he said dismissively. "She hit someone."

Yu Ling looked at Kuan Kuan. She'd had no idea he knew too. "You're as bad as your mother," she snapped, and came back down the steps to thrust the keys at Xiaomin. She stalked into the house without looking back, walking quickly as if she was afraid they would come after her. Even after they were out of view, she couldn't slow down.

It happened fifteen years ago, not long after she got her license. She'd carried the document in its black plastic wallet everywhere with her. As the first female professional driver in her town, she had every reason to be proud, particularly as she'd gotten the B2 heavy vehicle license and had been hired by a local trucking firm. She would start in a month, basically taking over her father's job. Although he still had two years till retirement, he hadn't been the same since his prostate cancer surgery, and could no longer sit for long periods. No one wanted to come out and say it, because the family knew how stubborn he could be. He hated admitting to weakness, and insisted on soldiering on. That day, he'd taken on a job delivering some furniture. Because it was long-distance, Yu Ling's mother asked her to go along, though they both knew she probably wouldn't get to do any driving. Asking her father to take the passenger seat would definitely send him into a rage. He hated having anyone else take the wheel, let alone his own daughter. He'd looked down on her ever since she was a little girl. She'd learned to drive a truck to show him she was more useful than most girls, but that didn't have much effect on the way he treated her.

Afterward, her mother asked over and over, *Did your father make you do it?* She shook her head no. He hadn't so much as hinted at it. Yes, he loved giving orders indirectly, but not that night.

She'd dozed off in the passenger seat and was woken by a violent jolt. It was dark out. First they saw plastic bottles scattered across the ground, then the man lying among them. Her father immediately turned into a helpless, blubbering mess. His tears tormented Yu Ling, and she felt she had to do something. If she hadn't fallen asleep, she could have kept a lookout and this would never have happened. Before the police arrived, she'd decided to make a sacrifice that her spoiled little brother would never have been capable of.

The police bought her story. After all, she was a new driver. The court didn't take long to sentence her. The deceased was a sixty-four-year-old scrap collector with no family who lived in a cheap rented room in an urban village. During her second year in prison, her father's cancer returned and he died a few months later. Her mother said it was the dead man who'd taken him away.

Yu Ling never touched a steering wheel again. At first she'd thought all that would happen was she'd have to give up being a trucker. After getting out of jail, she realized that wasn't the half of it. This would be a stain on her for the rest of her life.

Finding a decent job in her county would no longer be easy, and even her love life was affected. When things were getting serious with a boyfriend, she worked up the courage to explain to him what she'd done that night. He was utterly confused, and thought if what she was saying was true, there must be something wrong with her. Opening up to him didn't bring them closer. In fact, it pushed them apart, and marriage was no longer in the cards. She felt foolish and resolved never to tell another soul. Fortunately, she was able to move farther and farther from her hometown, until she reached a place where no one knew her past. That is, until she was refused a US visa, and Qin Wen got someone to look into her background.

Yu Ling kept thinking back to the evening she'd offered to resign. She hadn't planned to give any kind of explanation, but standing there, she'd felt molten lava roiling within her. Out of nowhere came the sensation that if she told the truth, Qin Wen would trust her. She believed their connection transcended the employer-employee relationship. It wasn't as simple as one of them paying the other to work.

"I'm sorry I kept this from you, I didn't mean anything bad by it," she'd said by way of explanation. Then she couldn't stop herself from adding, "I didn't do it. Do you believe me?"

"They must have had their reasons for sending you to jail," Qin Wen said. Who was "they"? Why did "they" have to come between her and Qin Wen? Qin Wen was reclining on the velvet couch, flipping through an auction catalog. Her face was a frosty blank, as if determined to keep this purely a work matter. That expression kept appearing before Yu Ling's eyes long afterward, causing her shame. She understood how ridiculous she'd made herself with this one-sided baring of her soul.

Yu Ling walked through the main gate of Golden Lake Villas and headed for the bus stop. The sky was overcast and willow-seed puffs danced through the air. She hadn't decided where she was going, but no matter her destination, she'd need to take this bus. Perhaps she could visit Mrs. Wu? She needed to find a place where she could rest and regain the strength to make longer-term plans.

"Nanny Yu!" called someone behind her.

She froze. Engine rumbling, a black SUV pulled up beside her. The window slowly wound down, and a young woman with long black hair took off her sunglasses. Miss Amy.

"Such a coincidence, I was on my way to your place," said Miss Amy. Then, cautiously, "Is Kuan Kuan home alone? Is anyone with him?"

"A friend of his father's," said Yu Ling. "You can talk to her about Kuan Kuan."

"Are you headed to the store? I can give you a lift."

Yu Ling shook her head and kept walking. The SUV followed slowly behind her, but she ignored it. When she sat at the bus stop, it stopped there too.

"You've passed it, the main gate is that way."

"Yes, I saw." Miss Amy leaned from the window. "I'm

actually here to see you. Can we talk, Nanny Yu? Are you in a hurry?" She looked expectantly at Yu Ling.

In the last year, Yu Ling had sold every minute of her time, not even resting on New Year's Eve. Now all she had was time, but she didn't know what to do with it.

"No, I'm not in a hurry."

know you're angry with me," said Miss Amy. "I shouldn't have said all that to you."

They were in the outdoor seating section of a restaurant, the only customers there, probably due to the gray sky and howling wind. A server was busy clearing away remnants of a birthday celebration from the day before, scraping gold foil lettering off a window. On the grassy patch before them, LED lights in the shape of a 5 still shone, with a shriveling balloon arch over them like an unpromising vineyard. In the distance, a waiter was running after a stray balloon that the wind tossed this way and that. All of a sudden, Yu Ling remembered she'd been here before, for someone else's birthday party: Andy, one of Kuan Kuan's classmates. Jianni, Xiaoliang, and Eva had been there too. She realized that she could remember the names of almost all his classmates, all his teachers, his roommates at summer camp, and the young man they'd met at the science center. Her brain was full of useless information, and she had no idea how she could clear it out once and for all. It was a question of time. Perhaps the day would come when she'd no longer be able to recall Kuan Kuan's name.

Miss Amy insisted on buying her breakfast, so Yu Ling ordered a bagel with smoked salmon and English breakfast tea. The portions were larger than she'd expected. Her bagel was topped with two poached eggs, like white goggles on a plump child. The server brought them coffee and tea, and even when she stepped to one side, her back remained ramrod straight. She'd probably just arrived in Beijing and hadn't yet learned how to cut corners, as Yu Ling's mother would say.

"I only found out later what happened to Kuan Kuan's family," said Amy. "I think I owe you an apology. I'm sorry."

"No need." Yu Ling kept her eyes fixed on her cup as she swirled her tea bag.

Nobody had ever said "I'm sorry" to her. When she was little, her mother had given the best of everything to her brother, then said to her, *This is hard on you, I know.* There'd been an apology in those words, but also the implication that this was how things were, that she ought to understand. No one ever said sorry in their village. Everyone thought if their actions weren't illegal, they couldn't be truly harmful. As long as the wound wasn't visible, no one needed to take responsibility. Yu Ling agreed with this way of thinking, and had been confused at the way Qin Wen frequently demanded apologies from Kuan Kuan. *You did something wrong, didn't you? What should you say?* Qin Wen would nag until Kuan Kuan said, "I'm sorry." What good did *sorry* do? Could it change anything? An empty ritual. Yet at this moment, now that someone had said the words to her, Yu Ling felt as if she'd been stung by an insect. Her eyes prickled, and she felt a burst of resentment, not because of anything Amy had done, but from years and years of past grievances, so many she couldn't have named any specific one.

"You could have walked away, couldn't you? Who would blame you, in these circumstances?" Miss Amy was saying, getting herself all worked up. "But you stayed by Kuan Kuan's side. This must all have been such a violent blow to him. You must know what a difference your companionship made."

"I haven't told the child. He doesn't know anything about this."

"That was the right thing to do, and so was keeping him home from school. We needed a bit of time to make preparations before he comes back. We have psychiatrists on staff now, they'll be working with me." Miss Amy looked solemn, like she was about to embark on some great undertaking. "That is, assuming Kuan Kuan doesn't change schools. Is he going to? What I'm trying to say is, putting him in a new environment at a time like this might make the situation worse." She gave Yu Ling a look. "Of course, that's not our decision. All we can do is pray that his family isn't guilty of anything worse."

Amy had only eaten half her croissant. She asked the straight-backed waitress for another Americano.

"How do you feel about this?" Amy ran her finger round the rim of her cup.

"About what?"

"When you found out about their corruption, all that money they took—" She lowered her voice. "Do you think less of them now? Do you feel differently about your job, or even about Kuan Kuan?"

"No. This whole business has nothing to do with me."

"I see."

"That's just what government officials do, isn't it? Why else would anyone want those jobs?"

Amy's face stiffened, but quickly relaxed again. "If you'd said that to me before, I'd have become very angry. I used to lose my temper whenever anyone thought differently from me. But I'm doing better now. I was too arrogant. Why did I think I knew it all?"

It was strange to hear Amy talking about herself like this.

"I read a novel," she went on, "about a butler who spent half his life serving a gentleman he thought was good and righteous. Then in the end he found out his master had been helping the Nazis." She paused, scrutinizing Yu Ling for a reaction. "You know, the Nazis? The bad guys who started the war and killed innocent people? The butler was very disappointed, no, not just disappointed, he was ashamed. He felt he'd wasted his life, and the stain it left on him could never be wiped away."

"At least his master paid his wages," said Yu Ling.

"Yes, but a lot of people could pay your wages, and you can only work for one of them. Naturally you hope your labor will go toward something of value. It's the same with a country, you're loyal to your nation because you hope it will provide for all its people, and not just the powerful or the ruling class . . ."

"Did he have children?"

"What?" Amy looked annoyed at being interrupted.

"Did the butler take care of the gentleman's children?"

"Well . . ." Amy thought about it. "The book doesn't mention any other family members, so I guess he didn't have a wife or kids."

"It would be different if there was a child. You watch a child grow up day by day, that's your achievement. You'd never feel you'd completely wasted your time."

"That's true." Amy pondered her words and smiled. "Now I understand why I felt there was something missing in the novel. You're right, it would be completely different if there was a child. Even the children of the Nazis were innocent and deserved to be treated well. Children dissolve any kind of opposition. Maybe that's why I chose to stay here and keep doing this job. I believe I can change the kids for the better, even a little. That's the most real thing. No matter what happens in the world tomorrow, no one could deny that my job is meaningful. Don't you agree?"

Yu Ling shrugged, and Amy smiled again.

"We women get emotional so easily. One of my male bosses said to me, the reason the female revolutionaries were the most fervent is that they lived in a fantasy, always believing they stood center stage playing the lead role. That's why they seemed afraid of nothing.

"By the way, Nanny Yu, I have a friend who's a journalist at a British newspaper. He's working on an in-depth piece about government corruption and wants to interview someone who can give a perspective that Western readers haven't heard before. I think you'd be perfect. Would you be willing to speak to him?"

"Forget it. I don't know anything, and I'm not good at talking. I won't say anything interesting."

"All right, let me know if you change your mind. He's a really passionate reporter. He'll be heading back to the UK this summer."

Unnecessarily, Yu Ling noticed that the ring on Amy's fourth finger was no longer there.

As they left the restaurant, the server was returning with some of the runaway balloons he'd managed to capture.

"Can I have one?" said Yu Ling. The straight-backed waitress ran over and placed all the strings in Yu Ling's hand, a dozen or so.

"Have them all! Thanks for stopping by!"

Miss Amy insisted on giving Yu Ling a lift, and asked where she wanted to go. Yu Ling thought about it and said back to Golden Lake Villas. From the passenger seat of the SUV, she could barely tell the windscreen was there. When a parasol tree branch fell in front of them, she felt as if it would stab right through her. At the next junction, Amy glanced at the red-light countdown and swung the steering wheel around with her slender arms, causing the vehicle to swerve left as she stepped on the gas. The balloons in the rear seat shook violently, and a blue one bobbed into the gap between them.

"Slow down!" Yu Ling made a grab for the balloon.

As they approached the house, she spotted Kuan Kuan sitting on the front steps with his head on his knees. Hearing the engine, he looked up in their direction, but didn't recognize the SUV. His head sank again. Yu Ling wound down her window and called to him. He jumped to his feet and ran into the middle of the road.

"Watch out!" Yu Ling cried.

"You look like you're doing okay, young fella." Amy jumped out and pushed her sunglasses to the top of her head. Kuan Kuan walked over and took Yu Ling's hand. His lower lip trembled, like he was about to cry.

"Here. These were the only colors they had." Yu Ling knelt and handed him the balloons, looping the strings a couple of times around his wrist.

"I shouldn't have said you're a bad driver. I'll never do it again," Kuan Kuan whispered, flinging his arms around her. She felt his warm breath against her ear. When she hugged him back, she felt him give her his entire weight. She didn't know what would happen next, but she was sure of one thing: right now, he needed her. Not the way a child needs a nanny, but more—something like *family*. Everyone at the train station had heard them call her that, which made it feel real.

23

Yu Ling and Kuan Kuan went back inside. Xiaomin was lying on the couch staring at the ceiling, but sat up when she heard them and clicked off the TV.

"He insisted on waiting outside for you. I couldn't drag him back in." She stood and followed Yu Ling into the kitchen. Once again, she rotated her wrists. "Kuan Kuan needs you, I see that now. Everyone else can leave, but you have to stay."

"Oh? Shouldn't I have my own life?"

"Of course, just not right now." Xiaomin jumped to touch the top of the doorframe. "Yafei was on the news again today. He's accused of using his father-in-law's position for improper gain." She let out a breath. "This seems serious."

"It's only been a couple of days. You've already changed your mind?"

Kuan Kuan appeared in the doorway. "Excuse me, I need to borrow Auntie Xiaomin." He took her hand and they ran out.

That afternoon, as Yu Ling was tidying up the house, Dalei

phoned. He didn't mention Donghu or the van, he only wanted to say he was bringing over a couple of crates of fruit. For free, he added, a fringe benefit from the supermarket he worked at. Yu Ling told him not to bother, but he insisted. He knew things must be tough, and he wanted to help out. Finally, she accepted because it seemed rude to keep saying no, and asked if he could also bring seeds—she wanted to start a vegetable garden.

In the evening, she went into the living room and found it in darkness, apart from the strings of Christmas lights surrounding the tent, the persimmon-seed bulbs glowing then dimming, as if they were breathing. The balloons were tied to the four corners of the tent. Kuan Kuan and Xiaomin came stumbling down the stairs, carrying a box between them. Kuan Kuan asked Yu Ling not to come in yet, they weren't done decorating.

The doorbell rang: Duomei and the little girl again. Duomei's leggings were magenta today. As usual, the girl squirmed past Yu Ling and ran into the house calling Kuan Kuan's name.

"You look more and more like you own this place." Duomei opened the plastic folder in her hands and flipped through the papers inside. Indicating with her finger, she handed it to Yu Ling. "Sign here, please."

In bold black lettering, it read, "Golden Lake Villas dog ownership regulations (amended)." Duomei pointed out where it said the new neighborhood committee had voted to cancel the time restrictions on dog walking. Thinking she was being asked to sign on Qin Wen's behalf, Yu Ling refused.

"Sign your own name, as a representative of Unit 201-101. You live here, so you have the right to make that call. Qin Wen's been removed from the neighborhood committee."

Duomei shut the folder. "Any news from her?" When Yu Ling said no, she didn't seem disappointed, as if she'd only asked the question to pave the way for her own revelations. She'd heard her ma'am say someone had spotted Qin Wen buying toilet paper at an Asian supermarket in San Francisco. Also, Hu Yafei had a mistress whose father and brother owned several publicly traded companies that relied on Qin Xinwei's backing, and now the mistress was on the run too.

"Plenty of rich people have done shameful things. The more respectable they seem, the more dirty laundry they have. Huh, they're so afraid of being exposed, they won't let the rest of us see daylight." Then she started talking about the dog again, how she'd finally be able to take him for a walk during the day, stepping out proudly with that old mutt. Yu Ling thought if Duomei could only take one thing from her employers' home, she'd probably choose the dog.

Later, as Yu Ling made dinner, Xiaomin came into the kitchen to ask if she needed help. Yu Ling passed on all of Duomei's gossip, particularly the part about Hu Yafei's mistress being on the run, watching Xiaomin closely for a reaction.

Xiaomin's tall body began quivering. "Oh no, that's not me! I'm not the mistress! Do I look like my family owns businesses? I can show you my savings account, I still haven't paid last month's credit card bills!" She opened the fridge and grabbed a bottle of seltzer, which she pressed to her cheeks, breathing deeply.

"I was planning to leave anyway, I might as well tell you the truth. I'm not Yafei's girlfriend. Nothing's happened between us."

Yu Ling glanced at her, then went back to chopping vegetables. "You're afraid of getting dragged down too, I suppose."

"Go ahead and call the police, see if they arrest me. Sure, I lied to you, but I ended up paying for stuff out of my own pocket. That's not illegal, is it?"

"Who the hell are you, then?"

"I . . . I'm Hu Yafei's trainer. He goes to UJoy gym, yes? Usually in the morning, occasionally in the afternoon, never in the evening. I'm right, aren't I? That morning, I was standing right next to him when he found out about Qin Xinwei. He made a few phone calls, canceled our session, and left in a hurry. When the news came out, I heard another member say he'd been taken away for questioning."

She opened the bottle and glugged half of it down.

"I really did like him. He's so refined, and he's nice to everyone. If he hadn't booked a hundred sessions with me up front, I'd probably have been fired by now. I'm not great at my job. I'm sloppy when I demonstrate the moves, and I keep getting distracted. Sometimes I lose track when I'm counting reps because I've started wondering what to have for lunch. Yafei said this helped him feel less stressed, because he could let his mind drift too. He helped me out last year: My ma was diagnosed with lung cancer and came to Beijing for surgery, but after two months she still hadn't managed to get an appointment. I was on the phone trying to get her wait-listed, and Yafei overheard. He told me to hang on and made one phone call. That evening, the hospital got in touch to let me know they'd admitted my ma. Soon after that, she had her operation, and the lead surgeon was the head of internal medicine! My first thought was:

This is probably worth a hefty bonus! I didn't know how this sort of thing works, so I phoned to ask him how much I ought to give, and he said I didn't owe anyone anything. I kept trying to buy him dinner, but he kept refusing. He said this was nothing to him. And now he's in trouble, I can't just stand by, can I? That day on the phone, he kept talking about Kuan Kuan, as if that was the hardest thing for him, so I came. No matter what, you have to admit I've helped."

"You could just have helped. Why pretend to be his lover?"

"If I hadn't, would you have let me near the child? Besides, when he gets out of jail and sees I've been looking after his son, he might be so touched that we really do end up together, and then we can move to the States."

"Ah, so that's the main point. You want to use him to get to America."

"We don't have to get married. He owns property and businesses over there, he could easily sponsor a visa."

"What's so great about America? I saw on TV that they're always having shootings. Chinese people get shot dead over there."

"You ought to see it for yourself. They're always going on vacation there—didn't they ever bring you?"

"I don't want to go. I'm not going anywhere."

"It's not that everything is wonderful over there, I just got hung up on it. When I was younger, I represented China in a tournament. We were there for half a month. One night, I snuck out of our dorm to get something to eat, but I got lost and couldn't find my way back. I tried asking an old guy I saw at a gas station. I hardly spoke any English, so I had to mime. He said he'd drive me, and we ended up going in circles all night until I spotted our building. It was almost dawn. The old guy got all excited when I said I was an athlete, and came to see the match. When we won, he said it was all down to his delivering the star player. We agreed that the next time I was in town for a game, he would bring me to see Red Rock Canyon in a helicopter. But the year after that, I busted my knee and had to leave the team."

"What sport?"

"Volleyball. I was an amazing opposite, there wasn't a shot I couldn't block. The old guy's probably dead by now. I hung on to his phone number, but I never called him." She tossed the empty bottle in the trash. "It's probably time for me to leave."

"That was some good acting, you could have kept playing the part," said Yu Ling.

Xiaomin shook her head and confessed that she'd already seen the rumors online, and had been sad to learn that Hu Yafei had a real-life mistress. She'd sensed for some time that his marriage was going south, otherwise she'd never have tried to insert herself into the picture. Yafei had told her his wife was never satisfied no matter what he did, and she didn't like children. The main reason she was giving up on her romance with Yafei wasn't because of the mistress, though, but because she now knew the situation was more complicated than she'd imagined. She'd thought Yafei was just implicated in someone else's wrongdoing, but now he was being accused of a serious crime himself, and the government would probably confiscate all his property. It was hard to say if he'd ever get back to the States. Also, during the few hours when Yu Ling was gone, she'd learned that she didn't have the ability to look after a child on her own.

"Do you think Kuan Kuan will be upset if I leave?"

"Don't flatter yourself. Kids forget fast."

"Really? He told me when he was five, he got separated from you at an amusement park. He remembered every detail—it's like I was there. You told him if it ever happened again, he should stay put and not go running around."

A jolt shot through Yu Ling's head. To think she'd almost made use of this incident to abandon the boy at that same amusement park. She bent over her work and didn't say anything for a while. Xiaomin came up behind her and gently tapped her shoulder.

"Hey, you're the world's greatest nanny."

Yu Ling stared at her in shock, and Xiaomin burst out laughing. "The old American guy taught me how to give compliments. Praise is its own language, and it's universal!" Then, more seriously, "But sometimes the compliments are true. I really do think that."

Yu Ling turned back to wiping the wet countertop. "When are you leaving?"

Xiaomin shrugged. "I'll start packing now."

"At least stay for dinner."

Kuan Kuan appeared in the kitchen doorway and solemnly announced that Swan Home was now wired for electricity.

That evening, dinner was yellow croaker stir-fried with glutinous rice cakes, char siu pork, and lotus root stir-fried with ginkgo and snow peas. At Xiaomin's fervent request, Yu Ling also grilled a steak. When she turned off the gas and brought the soup in, the living room was utterly silent. Xiaomin and Kuan Kuan stood in front of the tent. Yu Ling asked what was happening, but Kuan Kuan put a finger to his lips and waved her over. The orangey-red light shone on the tent flap, illuminating the wooden Welcome sign. Inside were a small coffee table with a teapot and four cups, and a mat with a neatly folded blanket. Between them was the goose, elongating its neck to investigate its surroundings.

"It went in on its own?"

Kuan Kuan nodded. "Swan Home finally has a guest!"

Xiaomin said, "Why don't we leave our guest to get settled in, and go have dinner?"

After the meal, they went back to Swan Home and found the visitor had departed. Through the window, Yu Ling saw it back in the yard, pacing around its empty food bowl. She grabbed a baby napa cabbage, plucked off some leaves, and went outside to toss them to the goose. On her way back in, she noticed one of the tiles from the gazebo roof was lying on the ground, smashed. Moving closer, she saw the ball-shaped surveillance camera was gone.

Who had done this? Her heart thumped violently. It was completely dark. She looked around the yard, retreated a few steps, and hurried back into the house.

24

A short while after that, the goose began honking in the yard. Kuan Kuan ran to the window and saw it had jumped onto the gazebo railing, where it was flapping its wings in a panic.

"It's flying!" He pressed his face to the window. "I knew it could fly!" He flung open the door and tried to run out, but Yu Ling pulled him back.

"Don't scare it, or it might not be able to fly anymore."

She brought the boy upstairs for his bath, told Xiaomin to keep him company, and found them a couple of water pistols to do battle with. Going back down alone, she peered out into the yard from the back door. The goose had run off to the far end of the garden, still thrashing its wings and craning its neck toward the gazebo.

Yu Ling went to the kitchen, drank a glass of water, and got a rolling pin from the drawer. With this in her hand, she turned off the living room lights and headed out into the backyard.

The goose was about to charge the gazebo, chest puffed out, but when it saw her striding over, it swiftly turned around, rump waggling as it retreated to the garden wall. The air was crisp, and dank gloom clung to the tall magnolia tree, which rustled in the wind. Yu Ling tiptoed around the rock formation, round the back of the gazebo, where someone was huddling. The figure leaped up just as she caught sight of it and flung some sort of bundle at Yu Ling as it fled. Prepared for this, Yu Ling managed to grab hold of the intruder and bring the rolling pin down hard on their back. The figure screamed.

"It's me!" In the murky moonlight, the woman frantically pushed her hair back from her face. "It's me, Yu Ling. It's me."

And Yu Ling saw that the figure before her was indeed her ma'am, Qin Wen.

Qin Wen followed Yu Ling back into the house. She moved slowly, limping with her right leg. Her trousers were ripped on that side, the shredded fabric trailing on the carpet. She wore a dark green silk blouse she'd been very fond of, now snagged and covered in loose threads, with a white sweat stain across the chest. Her hair was greasy and matted, plastered stickily to her scalp, making her face look weird, almost square. She stopped to lean against the couch, screwing up her eyes as they adjusted to the light.

"What, you don't recognize me anymore?" she said with a frosty smile when she noticed Yu Ling staring. Her face stiffened and her eyebrows shot up. "A goose? Where did that come from?"

"Kuan Kuan wanted it. Would you like some warm water?" Yu Ling headed into the kitchen.

"Where's Kuan Kuan? How's he doing?" Qin Wen followed her, sounding a little tearful. Yu Ling said the boy was upstairs, should she bring him down?

"In a while," said Qin Wen. "Let me wash my face first, I don't want to frighten him." She limped toward the bathroom. Yu Ling thought she probably wasn't so much trying to protect the boy as unable to bear being seen like this.

She had to admit that as she watched Qin Wen slowly limping from the backyard into the house, she'd thought how tragic her situation was and wondered how she could bear it. Yet ever since she was a child, Yu Ling had seen and heard about many women in far more dire straits, going mad or losing their voices, being sold into arranged marriages or getting locked up in chains. "That's how it is with women, no matter what kind of lives you give us, we'll survive," her mother would say after recounting yet another story about an unfortunate woman, her tone a little sarcastic but also full of pride. Or perhaps she was simply stating a truth. In any case, Qin Wen wasn't someone who could survive any kind of life you gave her. Yu Ling stood at the water dispenser thinking about all the news reports she'd read online about the wives of government officials killing themselves after their husbands got arrested. These women invariably chose to die at home, locking themselves in tiny rooms and tossing a rope over a rafter or slicing open a vein. Yu Ling tried to recall the layout of the bathroom, whether there were any sharp objects in the cabinet under the sink. Abruptly, she turned off the faucet and hurried out with the half-full glass.

Qin Wen was sitting at the dining table, gobbling down the leftover steak on Kuan Kuan's plate. Her cheeks bulged and she chewed effortfully, meat juices dripping from her lips and pooling on her chin. Next, she reached for the char siu pork that Xiaomin had been saving for a midnight snack. With her greasy hand, she took the glass and gulped a mouthful of water, only to choke on it and start coughing violently, her whole face flushing red. Yu Ling went over and thumped her back. After a long while, she quieted down, but tears continued to stream from her reddening eyes, more and more of them. She covered her face with her hands and wept.

"I had to walk back. I didn't have any money. They wouldn't let me on the train, and I only managed to get a ride part of the way. The rest of the time, I walked. Through the night, every waking moment. My shoes are ruined, my feet are covered in blisters. The day before yesterday, it rained all day and I took shelter under a bridge. There were four or five homeless people there too, one of them had an amputee child with her. I didn't want to sleep there, but I couldn't walk another step. I dreamed that Kuan Kuan and the disabled child were the same person, Kuan Kuan's face on the child's body, speaking with Kuan Kuan's voice, *Mama, what's wrong?* When I woke up, I couldn't stop crying. I was so worried something had happened to him." She slumped on the table, sobbing so hard she couldn't speak. After some time, she lifted her head and took Yu Ling's hand. "You have no idea. When I came back and saw there was someone here, my heart was filled with such gratitude. I was afraid you'd have left, that you'd have abandoned Kuan Kuan."

"How could I do that?" Yu Ling pulled her hand free. "Where did you walk from? Weren't you in Hong Kong?"

"I didn't dare take a plane. I went to Luohu and crossed the border into Shenzhen. After Yafei got taken, they froze our bank accounts so I couldn't get any money. I transferred five hundred yuan to someone on my phone and they gave me cash. Then I got scared they would track my phone and threw away my SIM card. I took long-distance buses. By the time I got to Tianjin, I'd spent all my money."

"Did you smash the camera outside? Do you think they're watching this place?"

Qin Wen lowered her voice. "They can't know I'm back. No one can know, understand?"

Then they heard someone humming a tune. Huang Xiaomin was coming down the stairs.

25

Qin Wen jumped up and tried to run for the door, but her injured leg slowed her down. She gave up and turned to stare at Xiaomin, bemused by her appearance: swathed in a bathrobe, steam rising from her substantial frame, face bright red, hair scooped into a small bun atop her head, large pink ears protruding Buddha-like.

"Who's this?" Xiaomin said casually, looking Qin Wen up and down.

Yu Ling said this was Kuan Kuan's mother.

"Oh, wow." Xiaomin gaped in shock.

Qin Wen looked at Yu Ling, waiting for her to complete the introduction.

"Mama!" The boy appeared at the staircase landing.

Qin Wen was perfectly still. By the time she managed to turn, the boy had come down the stairs, droplets of water glistening in his hair.

"Kuan Kuan!" She knelt and spread her arms wide. As she

folded the boy into herself, tears began trickling down her face. "Are you okay, sweetheart? Is everything okay?" She lifted his face and kissed his forehead.

"I'm doing great, Mama. I have a swan. Would you like to see it?"

"Oh, a swan, very good. I think I saw it out in the yard." Her eyes roamed over Kuan Kuan's features.

"But you haven't been to Swan Home yet," said the boy eagerly. "It's over there. Come and see?"

"Maybe later, darling, I'm a bit tired now." She pinched his arm. "I think you've gotten bigger."

"That's right, Mama, I grew up last Sunday. That's the day we met the swan. The uncle with the truck had a whole load of them. I want to rescue them all. Can I?"

"Of course." She stood up wearily, then tensed again when her eyes fell on Xiaomin, who was wearing Qin Wen's Egyptian cotton bathrobe. She'd probably helped herself to the bathtub with the massage jets and the orange blossom bath oil Qin Wen had bought in Paris. But why was her hair dripping wet? Why not use the ionic dryer on the marble counter?

"I'm Yu Ling's friend, I came to help out," said Xiaomin. "Kuan Kuan had a fever and she couldn't leave him, so I ran some errands, got groceries and so on. Oh, and I bought some of those pastries Kuan Kuan loves. Ridiculously expensive. I paid for them!"

"You had a fever!" Qin Wen hugged the boy again, but this time he wriggled free.

"Since you're back, I don't think I'm needed here." Xiaomin waved goodbye. "No need to thank me. I came here because of my friendship with Yu Ling, and I really get on well with Kuan Kuan. Even if we met in the street, I think we'd still become buddies." She put her strapping arm around Kuan Kuan and gave him a squeeze, chin to his cheek, pretended to pull his pigtails, and gave him a couple of smacks on the bum. Kuan Kuan shot off like a rocket, sprinted twice around the room, then collapsed rigidly onto the floor, announcing that his batteries were flat.

"How did he get a fever?" Qin Wen turned to Yu Ling. "That was careless, it's not like you." Her voice was reproachful and a tiny bit rueful, as if it was unthinkable that her nanny could get such a simple thing wrong. Yu Ling wondered what sort of response she was expecting. An apology? She sensibly didn't try to explain herself. Whenever Qin Wen got an excuse from someone she was scolding, she'd put on a disappointed look and say she wasn't interested in hearing that, it didn't mean anything to her. "I just want to know that you understand your mistake, got it?" Qin Wen never made mistakes herself, she was like an alien being from a superior planet, forced to live amongst flawed humans, taking on the responsibility of helping them to grow. Hearing this familiar tone, Yu Ling let out a sigh of relief. If Qin Wen still had the strength to blame her, that probably meant she wasn't going to despair and end it all.

"Time you were in bed." Yu Ling tried to lift Kuan Kuan from the floor, but he shook off her hand and ran to the end of the corridor, where he quietly pulled open the pet door. Yu Ling had shut it earlier to keep the goose out. Could he sleep in the tent, please? Qin Wen immediately said no, he'd definitely catch a cold if he did that. No matter how much Kuan Kuan promised he'd use a blanket and cocoon himself in the thickest sleeping bag, she still refused. The boy pressed himself to her legs, grabbing one of her arms and swinging back and forth.

"Please, Mama. Please!"

"Stop asking!" Qin Wen abruptly yelled, startling even herself. She took a moment to calm herself, then held Kuan Kuan's hand and said more quietly, "Darling, your baba is in trouble, it's up to me and you—" Her tears began flowing again, plopping onto the back of the boy's hand. "If you want to help your baba, head upstairs now and go to bed, all right?"

The boy followed Yu Ling up the stairs, suddenly quiet, not asking Yu Ling a single question. He washed up, got into pajamas, and lay down, staring at the ceiling. After some time, he said, "Auntie Xiaomin said when her mama was ill, my baba did her a big favor. My ba is a good person, isn't he?"

Yu Ling didn't know how to answer that. The boy shut his eyes. His chest rose and fell. Yu Ling understood that he would no longer tell her everything he was thinking. She placed her hand on his and pressed gently, then pulled the covers up to his chin.

26

Xiaomin was at the second-floor landing, dressed for travel and holding her suitcase.

"She's so beautiful, she's a good match for Yafei," she said with feeling as they walked down the stairs.

Qin Wen was still at the table, watching them descend. Yu Ling didn't feel like explaining anymore, so she walked Xiaomin straight to the front door. Behind them, Qin Wen called out, "I don't mind who you hang out with, I've always said you should go meet people from your hometown on your rest days, but this is a place of work, and every job has its requirements. You're supposed to put the child first, and—"

Xiaomin dropped her suitcase and stormed back into the kitchen. She went round the table, chose a plum from the fruit bowl, and bit into it. "Have you ever had a job?" she demanded. "I mean a real job. Have you ever been paid for your labor?"

Qin Wen's face turned pale. "I think it's time for you to go. You said you helped look after my child, and I'm grateful for that, but I imagine you've enjoyed our hospitality too. I'm exhausted, I need to rest. Yu Ling—"

"Ever since I was a kid, I've hated people telling me what to do." Xiaomin took aim and tossed the plum stone into the trash, then brushed off her hands and pulled out a chair. "By the way, do the police know you're here?"

Qin Wen's lips twitched. "I don't understand what you're trying to say."

"How about what's on the news? Do you understand that? Turn on the TV. Your father's been arrested, and so has your husband. Now they're looking everywhere for you."

"Why would they arrest me?" Qin Wen snapped. "I don't know anything."

Xiaomin picked up another plum and tossed it from hand to hand, turning to Yu Ling with a smile. "She says she doesn't know anything. Do you believe her? She lived in this enormous house, never lifted a finger, got waited on hand and foot as soon as she opened her eyes, had someone taking care of her child so she could go wherever she wanted—and she never once thought to ask where this life came from? Did it fall from the sky? Then how come it didn't crush us as it came down?"

"What the hell do you want?"

"I'm not sure, but I don't feel like leaving yet. You said I'd enjoyed your hospitality, so you won't mind if I have a drink, I suppose? Isn't there a lot of wine here?"

"Get her a bottle," said Qin Wen to Yu Ling.

"No, you go," said Xiaomin. "Everyone is equal here. Actually, no, you're beneath us, because you're a criminal and we aren't."

After a stunned moment, Qin Wen reluctantly stood and asked what Xiaomin preferred, white or red, dry or sweet. Xiaomin didn't have a preference, but made a show of thinking about it. "Something fruity, but not too fruity."

Moving very slowly, Qin Wen limped toward the wine cellar. Halfway there, she turned back to say, "I'm not a criminal."

Xiaomin patted the chair next to her, warmly inviting Yu Ling to sit down. In a low voice, she said, "It feels good to take the wind out of her sails, doesn't it?"

Yu Ling said nothing, which she later realized was a form of tacit agreement, even encouragement. Qin Wen came back and, as they watched, opened the bottle of red wine and poured two glasses, which she brought round to their side of the table.

On days when they had guests, Yu Ling was often pressed into service as a wine waiter. She'd learned how to decant it, how to choose the right glasses for a Burgundy versus a Bordeaux, how the wine they called "noble rot" was only to be served with dessert. She even remembered the drinking habits of repeat visitors. Some said they'd had enough when they actually wanted a little more, some kept asking for top-ups but needed to be cut off before they threw up. On these evenings, walking around the table with the decanter, she'd never imagined the day would come when she'd be sitting there with a glass of her own. Why would she want that? Wine didn't even taste good, and she had far more important, far more urgent things to yearn for. Those yearnings were gone this evening, though. She didn't need to think about anything at all, sitting at that shiny long table with a glass of wine that Qin Wen had poured her. Using the knowledge she'd acquired, she swirled her glass so the blood-colored liquid rose up the smooth sides like a rock climber, trying hard to cling to the surface. The longer it managed to linger there, the more expensive the wine.

Into her mind flashed the image of dinner guests swishing their glasses, as if each of them held a personal crystal ball, turning the future over in their hands. Where were these visitors now?

"So, tell me, why did you come back?" said Xiaomin, sounding like an interrogator.

In a low voice, Qin Wen said, "This is my home."

"Do you think you have a home at a time like this? You ought to have taken refuge in a hotel. I read online that there are hotels in Hong Kong with entire floors full of government officials escaping the Mainland."

"I told you, I don't know anything."

"Imagine pushing the blame for this onto everyone else and not taking any yourself. I feel sorry for your father and husband. I'm very kindly going to give you a little more time to think about your confession. If you're remorseful enough, I might be lenient for the sake of the child and consider giving you a way out." Xiaomin finished her wine and pushed the glass toward Qin Wen for more. "I can't tell if this is good or bad." She turned to Yu Ling. "Can you?" Then back to Qin Wen. "Wait, did you not bring me the best wine?"

Qin Wen's eyes were blank, as if she couldn't figure out what Xiaomin was saying. She sat very straight, clutching the decanter tightly, as if it were a balloon that would float free if she let go. After a long while, when they thought she wasn't going to answer, she said, "You asked me where my life came

from? It's true, I don't know." She smiled, almost apologeti-
cally. "Of course, it didn't just come to me out of nowhere, it
was a very slow process, changing bit by bit without me realizing it." She pursed her lips. "I remember in second grade, my
teacher suddenly started being extra nice to me. I got to be a
class cadre and help raise the flag at morning assembly. I
skipped my gym exam and still passed. On the last day of term,
she asked me to stay behind and said her husband wanted to
join the district education committee, could I ask my father to
have a word with the committee chair? I did as she asked, and
after that she treated me even better, sometimes so well it got
ridiculous. I didn't let her down, though. I wanted to deserve
this special treatment, so I studied even harder and got amazing grades. All my classmates wanted to play with me."

Xiaomin let out a frosty laugh. "How popular do you think
you'd have been, if your ba wasn't a big official?"

"He wasn't, though. Back then he was just the secretary to
the mayor, and no one thought he'd make it big. He was too
scholarly, too unworldly. Then when I was in junior high, he
got the promotion. He became a 'big official' with a secretary
of his own. After that he got so busy that if I wanted anything
from him, I had to ask his secretary, Mr. Du, who'd listen to
what I had to say and either he'd tell me no problem, or else
he'd say wait to hear from him—which meant he had to ask my
father. Mr. Du helped with my homework, came to parent-
teacher conferences, and bought me period pads. Because he
was a personal assistant, he had to deal with my father's personal life. Maybe he was more like a butler. Only a butler could
never become a master, whereas a secretary sometimes does

get promoted into the leadership. Mr. Du rose up the ranks with my father. One time I saw him at a ribbon-cutting ceremony. By then he'd gotten so imposing, I didn't dare say hello. I often wondered: When my father was a secretary, was he treated like Mr. Du, getting ordered around by his superiors' children? If those children could see him now, would they think he'd turned into a completely different person?" Qin Wen was frowning, her eyes fixed on a distant point, as if she were trying to see something clearly. "Then I realized why an English butler has such dignity: he never needs to plot how to turn into his master." She glanced at Yu Ling. "All right, I know this sounds unfair. What I mean is, people with fewer desires are much happier."

"You ought to take your own advice." Xiaomin tapped her glass twice, and Qin Wen immediately leaped to pour her more wine. She was adjusting quite well to her new position. Without waiting to be asked, she topped up Yu Ling's glass too.

"Do I have a lot of desires? I didn't want most of these things, they just naturally appeared around me. Anything I truly wanted, I couldn't have. I would have given up everything I owned for my mother not to die." She lowered her gaze and grimaced, as if she'd tasted something very bitter.

"She had a hereditary heart disease that made giving birth risky. Afterward, she was always sickly. Still, I never believed she would actually die. Then in my second year of high school, I was summoned from my boarding school. When I got to the hospital, she was surrounded by doctors. They told my ba she was getting better. Why couldn't they save her?" Her voice deepened. "I've always had this dark feeling that my dad never wanted her to get better. Maybe he told them to let her slip away. He already had a second wife in mind, a cadre. He said this was what the Party wanted. Maybe it was, because who could fall in love with a female cadre? They've all had to obey so many men on their way to the top, how could there be anything left in them that's truly theirs? My dad didn't mind. To him, women are all more or less the same. Which is why he's never had the sort of affair that would give them leverage over him. Don't misunderstand, I have nothing against my cadre stepmother. We get on fine as long as we stay out of each other's way. Anyway, I left the country as soon as I finished high school."

"Right, to the States," said Xiaomin.

Qin Wen looked surprised, or perhaps annoyed, that Xiaomin would know this about her, but she didn't pause.

"Let's talk about what you two care about most: money. I only started thinking about money in the States. That's when I abruptly realized I was a lot richer than the other overseas students. They could only afford to rent a room, I had an entire house. My dad didn't send me the money, it came from another uncle. At first I was uneasy about this arrangement, but I soon got used to it. After all, that logic had held since second grade: if my dad helped someone, it was only natural for that person to give him a little something in return. Anyway, that tiny amount of money was nothing to these people. So I stopped thinking about it. To a poor person, money is an individual issue, but for the rich, it's a family matter. As long as someone in your clan has access to money, you'll be fine. Not too much money, ideally, because that's when the trouble starts. My dad said that. He may have fallen from grace, but he's so intelligent, I don't think his enemies could have brought him down if he hadn't been unlucky. I don't know the details of his situation. My dad wouldn't let me touch politics. It's obvious why, isn't it? He believes women are prone to carelessness and we ruin things. He always said it was Madame Mao who ruined the Chairman's reputation. Of course, Madame Mao came to an even stickier end, so you could say he was protecting me. My husband and father always talked business alone. Whenever he came tó visit, the two of them would shut themselves away in the home office. Sometimes it felt like Yafei was my father's child, and I was the outsider." Qin Wen let out a long breath and tucked a stray hank of hair behind her ear.

"But Hu Yafei isn't your dad's child. If not for you, he wouldn't have gotten sucked into your family's affairs. He'd be fine now," said Xiaomin.

Qin Wen burst out laughing as if she might never stop, until tears came to her eyes. The decanter in her hands shook violently, the wine eddying right up to the rim.

"Is that what you think?" Qin Wen turned to Yu Ling. "Did you tell her that? Are you standing up for Hu Yafei?"

"I can't believe you're still complaining about your husband at a time like this," said Xiaomin. "I bet you think doing business is vulgar. He was never good enough for you."

The amusement drained from Qin Wen's face, leaving her despondent.

"Maybe I don't love him as much as I used to. Time grinds away at all sorts of things. You start to see a person differently. Even so, I definitely love him more than he loves me."

27

I t was love at first sight. I went to a friend's party and noticed
him as soon as I walked in. He was quiet all night, but no one
could ignore him. You couldn't say he was especially handsome,
but he had a sort of magnetism. You wanted to keep looking
at him."

Yu Ling noticed Xiaomin quietly nodding.

"He was five years older than me, and had worked for a
couple of years before coming to the States for his master's in
finance. He loved art, and we went to a lot of exhibitions in the
early days. Not just the two of us, of course, but all my attention was on him, not the rest of the group. One day, we went to
an Alice Neel show. Standing among her portraits, I had a sudden impulse to boldly pursue my own love. As we left the mu-
seum, I told him how I felt. He was quiet for a while, then he
said this was unexpected, and he needed time to think. He disappeared on me. I didn't hear from him for a whole month.
Just as I was thinking that was it, he resurfaced and said he'd

come to realize he loved me too. That's how we got together." Qin Wen stopped, savoring the moment. The creases on her forehead slowly smoothed out. "I was truly happy then. Really, I felt I was the happiest woman in the world." She laughed. "Whenever a woman thinks this, bad luck can't be far behind. So stupid.

"Soon he graduated, and couldn't find a job in the States. He wanted me to come back to China with him. This wasn't an easy decision, because I didn't want to keep living under my father's wing like a stupid pampered princess. In the end, I came back, and took him to see my father. My father had always hoped I'd find a husband from a similar background. Overseas, there's only a small circle of people as wealthy as us. Everyone knows everything about everyone else, and we support each other. Naturally, my ba wasn't pleased that Yafei came from an ordinary family. Is it strange that I enjoyed disappointing him? He was such a dictator, we all had to live under his thumb, and the only way to feel free was to go against him. Like the Monkey King squirming out from between the Buddha's fingers. It didn't take long till my father started appreciating Yafei. Such a hard worker, so eager to learn, he said. After dinner one night, Ba asked Yafei if he had any interest in working at a particular firm. Yafei tried to be blasé, but I could see he wanted it very much. Things were different from what I had imagined, but I still loved him. The day before our wedding, he finally told me the truth: He'd been married to a woman in Nanning, and they had a child together. After I told him I had feelings for him, he flew back to China to divorce her. He said he'd completely taken care of everything, the woman had full custody of the child, and I didn't need to worry about it. I was stunned. Now I understood what part my family background had played in our relationship, but it was too difficult for me to leave him then. You understand—I'd won, and it's hard to walk away from the card table when you're winning. Ba said I should accept him the way he was. Yafei and Ba were inextricably tied up in their business arrangements. My ba thought it was more important that Yafei was loyal to him than to me. Or maybe he believed that if he had Yafei's loyalty, then I would too."

Qin Wen put the decanter on the table and tilted her head to study the wine. "Our wedding was at an ancient castle in the south of France. That morning, my husband led a horse to where I was staying and helped me to mount. We went through a cave that echoed with the sound of rushing water, and arrived at a church on a hillside. It was my dream wedding, every detail. A priest officiated the ceremony, and although he was very well respected locally, I kept thinking he looked like an actor. When he bent over, his cross dangled in front of him. I had the urge to snatch it off. Poor priest. What had he ever done to me?"

"Wait, is this a Chen Shimei story?" asked Xiaomin.

"What, like the opera? No, in order to have a disloyal husband like Chen Shimei, you need a betrayed wife like Qin Xianglian. This story had a happy ending. His first wife didn't hate him at all, in fact she was the one who suggested the divorce and encouraged him to marry me. They both had a lot of siblings who needed their support, and this marriage could benefit all of them. Yafei liked to say his ex-wife was a principled woman. Heh. Just think about that, a woman sacrificing herself as a badge of honor! But there really are women who're willing to live within this delusion, and they're proud of it." She paused and puckered her lips, having reached the most bitter part. "I think they loved each other very much. They could end their marriage, but not their feelings for each other. The divorce strengthened their relationship. Yafei developed a lot of businesses in Guangxi, but always remained behind the scenes, and put his ex-wife's brothers and sisters in charge. His ex-wife wasn't involved much, she spent her time taking care of the child and her parents—as well as his parents, who still thought of her as their daughter-in-law. Everyone did as she said. She became like their matriarch, respected by all. Yafei went to see them every so often, and although he claimed it was his duty, I knew it was more like a need. Guangxi was the only place where he could be his true self, where he could actually relax. I often felt he was playing the part of my husband, and this was just a job to him, one with such a good salary that he couldn't refuse. Whenever he went back to Guangxi I would sneer: *What, another vacation?* He knew I looked down on him, but he didn't care until the day he realized his son looked down on him too." Qin Wen looked at Yu Ling. "You've seen it, haven't you? Whatever arrangements his ba makes, Kuan Kuan refuses to go along with them. He reflexively goes against his ba, he loves to provoke or embarrass him. No one taught him to be like that. No, I didn't. Yafei overestimated my influence on the child. To Kuan Kuan, neither of us is that important."

She turned her swollen eyes to Yu Ling. "I'm jealous, Yu Ling, that Kuan Kuan is so close to you."

Her gaze landed on the painting on the wall before her: a woman with her arm around a child's shoulder, holding him tight. A shudder went through her, as if she was coming back to herself.

28

"Something white just flashed past. Did the goose come indoors? Am I seeing things?"

"That goose is a VIP guest. It comes and goes as it pleases!" Xiaomin's face was flushed and her eyes were bloodshot. She staggered to her feet and chased the goose around the coffee table and armchairs. Finally, it hid behind a potted plant. She bent to pick a Lego brick off the carpet and lobbed it at the bird's head. The goose flapped its wings, squawking.

Qin Wen stood up. "The wine's finished. I'll go get another bottle."

"She shouldn't have any more."

"Who says?" Xiaomin made her way back to the table.

Qin Wen returned with more wine and poured it into a fresh decanter.

"So this first wife—is she the mistress they're talking about online?" Xiaomin rested her elbows on the table and allowed her head to slump into her hands.

"What mistress?" Qin Wen turned pale, but she calmed down as Xiaomin explained, mentioning the names of the woman's businesses. Yes, she said, that was the ex-wife.

"Have you met her?" asked Xiaomin.

"No. Do you think I should have? I've never even been to Guangxi. Maybe that's his real home, and this place is just a replica. One time I heard him on the phone buying antique furniture at auction, but it never got delivered here. So where did it go?"

"Why the hell didn't you just get a divorce?" said Xiaomin loudly. "What's stopping you?"

Qin Wen remained calm. "I did ask him for one. Not long after Kuan Kuan was born, I said we should separate because we weren't happy together. Yafei laughed and said our lives were fine, he didn't see any problems. He thought I must have read too many biographies of female artists, and that's why I wanted my life to be more dramatic. He was always saying, half jokingly, *Who but me would put up with you, my darling?* Whenever I was angry or sad or jealous, those words echoed in my ears and gradually lulled me into believing he was right. Nobody else would be able to stand me.

"Still, he's always supported me. He kept saying I ought to have my own art show." Qin Wen smiled wryly at Yu Ling. "That's right, a solo show. How many times have you heard us talking about that? He'd bring in a highly experienced curator from abroad, book the finest gallery, invite the most prominent people, throw the biggest opening party, and make sure all my paintings sold in no time at all. Did I want media coverage? I would have it. Recommendations from famous artists? No problem. Have my work collected by important museums? He could make that happen. I was different from other emerging artists, because there was nothing but success in my future! Wasn't that great? My husband never understood why I couldn't hurry up and finish all the paintings I was working on. The show was like a gift with no takers.

"The thing is, whenever I took up my brush and stood before a canvas, I'd think how the finished painting would probably end up in the cellar of some unbearably vulgar businessman that my husband happened to know, and the whole thing felt meaningless. They'd never hang it up, because I wasn't famous. These people don't think an object has value if they've never heard of it. The only reason they'd buy these paintings would be to curry favor with my father or husband. Who would want that kind of appreciation? Yet they wouldn't dare throw it away, because what if we came to visit? They'd need to hang it up then. Hence the cellar. I imagined introducing my work at my opening. My guests would pretend to be interested while actually thinking about something else. Who would care what I had to say? Would anyone believe I had any talent whatsoever? Do you, Yu Ling?"

"I don't understand art."

"You were always going through my catalogs in the studio."

"I was just tidying them up."

"Just admit it, you enjoy looking at paintings—but not mine. You must have thought to yourself, *She doesn't have a scrap of talent.*"

"I don't know what talent looks like. I've never bothered wondering about it."

"But Yu Ling, let me tell you, you're wrong. You might not believe it, but I was still in college when a gallery signed me. I took part in a group show, and the curator called me a rising star from Asia. I still have that catalog! I know I wasn't a genius, my talent only went so far, but I did have a little. Only later—it vanished. Or maybe it's still there, but I can no longer find it."

Her eyes were fixed on the painting before her. She murmured, "I wish there was nothing in my life but art."

"That's selfish," said Yu Ling. "You have Kuan Kuan too."

"If Alice Neel heard you, she'd reply: *To hell with the child.*"

"You should go to America," Xiaomin said out of the blue. "They'd like your paintings there."

"Really? You think so?" Qin Wen shook her head. "It's too late, anyway."

"Too late?" Xiaomin stared blearily in front of her, then without warning her head fell forward and she slumped over the table. A few seconds later, she started snoring loudly.

The other two women remained where they were, perfectly still. Lightning arced through the sky, turning it white for a moment. Thunder rumbled somewhere in the distance, followed by the sound of rain.

Qin Wen ran her finger over the table's wood grain. "I'm sorry," she said. "I shouldn't have said 'To hell with the child.' My child is adorable, and you take good care of him. I'm lucky to have had you here, all these years."

"If I wasn't here, where would I be?" said Yu Ling. She felt blood surging to her head.

Qin Wen looked surprised, then she smiled. "There are so

many places where you'd be needed. Mrs. Wu keeps asking me about you."

"If I left here, I could forget about finding another job. Isn't that what you said to me? Because you have leverage over me."

"I was just trying to make you stay. I don't have anything on you."

"What are you talking about? I killed a man."

"That wasn't your fault," said Qin Wen with certainty.

Yu Ling felt something slacken in her throat, and a faint moan emerged. A quiet, brief sound, scraping her throat like a slender chicken bone.

"It was your father behind the wheel. But you were in the vehicle, and you had a license—you'd just gotten it, hadn't you? So you took the blame, and did three years in jail. Your ma revealed what really happened when she was trying to have your record expunged."

"Two years and ten months."

"Right, you were a model prisoner, you even won a prize for your cloisonné craft. I've investigated you thoroughly, I know everything, I just never told you. I'm sorry, Yu Ling, that was wicked of me. I owe you an apology.

"You taking the fall for your father isn't any kind of leverage, but it does show your weakness: you're always sacrificing yourself for others. To be frank, I wanted to make use of that. Please forgive my selfishness, but after all, isn't that exactly the quality a nanny ought to have? A nanny has to build her life within someone else's, like a painting within a painting. Have you ever looked closely at one of those? You'd be surprised how crudely drawn they are, like undeveloped organs. Without a spirit of sacrifice, how could anyone maintain such a life? All these years, the affection you've had for Kuan Kuan is way more than a nanny should have. Can't you see that? Do you think I'm jealous that you occupy Kuan Kuan's heart? I'm also jealous that he's taken you away from me! Now all you think about is the child." She took Yu Ling's hand. "I've always comforted myself that at least you're happy. You always look so joyful playing with Kuan Kuan, I'd think to myself: Yu Ling's getting something out of this. She's not being forced to stay."

Yu Ling sat back in her chair. She removed her hand from Qin Wen's, wiped the tears from her cheeks, blew her nose, and stood up.

"I'll take her upstairs." She hauled Xiaomin to her feet, and draped Xiaomin's arm across her shoulders.

29

Yu Ling left Xiaomin in the guest bedroom. As she came back down the stairs, she heard the rain and saw it spattering against the round window at the landing. Raindrops kept hurling themselves against the glass, as if smashing themselves open to discover what they contained. The steady pattering surrounded the house. The air grew damp, heavy with drowsiness.

Yu Ling turned her gaze back indoors, and suddenly noticed one of the dining table chairs had gone missing. Then came the crash of a heavy object hitting the ground, followed by the goose honking. All she could see from her angle was the table with its wineglasses, decanter, fruit bowl, and a vase of blooming peonies. She hesitated, lacking the courage to take another step. She was afraid she would see a rope dangling from the rafters and those eternally fastidious eyes shut for good. The glassware glittered, making her recall the night she'd looked through the windshield and seen those bottles rolling across the road. At that moment, she'd prayed for the man not to be dead. She'd have willingly sacrificed something of her own for him to be alive. She did that anyway, taking the blame for her father, but it was too late. The trade-off didn't work, and she got nothing in return. Now she made another bargain with herself: as long as Qin Wen was unharmed, she'd make another sacrifice. But what of? What could she sacrifice? She didn't have very much. Still, she'd find something to give up. Her thoughts stopped at that "something," not daring to be more specific. Then rationality returned, and she hurried down the rest of the stairs. It had only been a few seconds, surely Qin Wen could still be saved.

Qin Wen was crouched down before the Alice Neel painting. The frame had been smashed, and jagged lengths of wood were scattered across the carpet. Yu Ling let out a breath. Qin Wen was muttering to herself about how flimsy the frame was, considering they'd only had it replaced a couple of years ago. Yu Ling almost quipped that they needed to find a new framing shop, this one was always using shoddy materials.

Qin Wen gathered the chunks of wood and examined them carefully on both sides before putting them down and turning her attention to the canvas, which she spread out on the floor. The woman in the painting looked startled to have her face pressed to the ground, like a suspect being arrested. Qin Wen gave her a pat-down, running her hands over the wooden backing. Finally, she picked up the scissors she'd placed by her side.

"Don't tell a soul what happened here today, all right?" She tried to prize off the brackets fastening the canvas to the board, but the scissors weren't sharp enough and only shaved off some splinters.

"What are you doing?"

"Do we have an axe?" Qin Wen went into the kitchen and came back with a long, slim knife, a muted silver blade that Hu Yafei had brought back from Kyoto. It was artisan-made, and could produce sashimi slices so thin they were translucent. Qin Wen plunged the knife into the wood. Yu Ling took a step forward, thinking she could help, but Qin Wen froze and eyed her warily until she could be sure she wasn't coming any closer. With an effort, she hacked off a bracket. Two screws fell to the ground, like little worms from an apple. The canvas was still fixed to its backing, so she started work on another bracket. By the time she got that off, the inner frame was covered in scratches. Finally the painting came free. Yu Ling thought she'd pick it up, but instead she held up the frame. Rising to her feet, she held it before her and ran a hand over its inside.

"It can't be. That's impossible." After she'd probed every inch of the wood, she shook it violently, hitting it on the ground as if to dislodge something. "Turn on the lights!"

Yu Ling hit the wall switch, and light poured into the room.

Qin Wen stared at the carpet, scanning the mazelike pattern of irises. Apparently no longer able to trust her eyes, she began running her fingertips over it.

"Yafei was standing on this spot that day. We'd just gotten back from a friend's place. He'd had a bit to drink. He was feeling down. Things were going south, he said, and there might be danger ahead. We couldn't keep hoping to be lucky, we needed some sort of insurance. When it was ready, he'd hide it behind this painting, and I could come get it if anything happened to him." Qin Wen was on her hands and knees, slowly moving across the carpet, brushing her palms over every inch.

"What does that mean, insurance?"

"Leverage. Wasn't that the word you used earlier? I'm talking about real leverage, something that would give me a hold over a government official who outranked my father. That night, Yafei said he might be able to obtain a recording of this man. It was evidence that the official had tried to intervene in the stock market. All I needed to do was contact him and say I had this tape, and he'd be forced to protect Yafei and my ba."

Qin Wen lifted the painting upright and began working away at the nails with the knife, trying to peel the canvas away from its backing.

"If Alice Neel knew about this—" Yu Ling heard herself say. Her first time saying a foreign woman's full name. Alice and Neel. They sounded like two names, like a couple.

Qin Wen paused, startled to hear this name in Yu Ling's mouth. She frowned at the picture, as if it no longer completely belonged to her. After a moment, she said frostily, "Alice Neel didn't know anything. Painting chose her, but it didn't choose me. My family chose me. Now my husband needs me, and so does my father. I'm the only one who can save them." She took a sharp breath, as if she'd just plunged her head into icy water, and continued working away at the nails. "He was different that day. Tender, like when we were first dating. He said I was the person he trusted most in this world."

The last nail came free, and the canvas slid off the wood onto the carpet.

Without the picture, the frame in her hands looked large as a doorway. She craned her head forward as if something was luring her through it, and pored over it, which didn't take long. It was picked clean, like bones. Then she laid out the painting. There were little folds at the corners, but they clearly held nothing.

Yu Ling watched Qin Wen fiddling with the painting. On many evenings, once Kuan Kuan was in bed, Yu Ling would come down to the kitchen to bake bread. When her dough was in the oven, she'd reward herself with a hot cup of tea. Holding the mug, she'd wander around the dining room, always stopping for a long while in front of this painting. A woman holding her child, fear and shock in her eyes, making the viewer want to know what she was looking at, what stood before her. And now Yu Ling saw her facing another woman, one who was shaking her violently, trying to make her hand over this lifesaving "leverage."

"It's got to be here somewhere." Qin Wen turned to Yu Ling. "Help me look. Maybe I missed it."

"What are we looking for?"

"I don't know. Maybe a thumb drive? It could be anything. A piece of paper with the location of a safety-deposit box, that sort of thing."

Yu Ling carried the painting with both hands to the couch and left it resting against a leather cushion. She joined Qin Wen in examining the frame once more, then knelt to scour the carpet inch by inch. They slowly broadened their search radius because Qin Wen said she thought she'd seen a few pieces of wood bounce away as she smashed the frame. They even looked under the sofa.

"How do you know this will actually work?" Yu Ling straightened up, leaning on one arm. "The big official might not care."

"Not possible. If this recording gets out, it'll ruin his entire life. Not just him—his family will be finished too, understand? They'll be forced to do as I say."

"Even if you get your way now, what if he takes revenge in the future?"

"I'll sit them all down and we'll negotiate. They won't want to cause a fuss either, that wouldn't do them any good." Qin Wen abruptly swung around. "The goose! It was here a minute ago. When I took apart the frame, it was right there, pecking at the fragments. I bet it ate the thing." She jumped up and scanned her surroundings. She and Yu Ling spotted the goose at the same moment: nibbling at the soil of a money plant. Moving as quietly as possible, Qin Wen inched in that direction, backing the goose into a corner. From behind the plant, it extended its neck, watching her warily.

Qin Wen looked down at the soil, then took a step back and bent to see if there was anything under the pot. Finally, she turned back. "It swallowed the thing."

"No way," said Yu Ling. "It would never eat anything like that."

"How would it know what it's eating? I saw with my own eyes, it came running over and pecked at the floor."

"That's a wild guess. Maybe this thing was never in the painting to start with."

"Impossible." Qin Wen picked up a long fragment of the frame that had a nail protruding from it. With her other hand, she grabbed the knife.

"What are you doing?" Yu Ling ran to block her way. "This has nothing to do with the goose. I told you, the thing you're looking for was probably never there."

Qin Wen's eyes were bloodshot. She shoved Yu Ling aside and ran over to the wall, blocking the escape route. Raising the board high, she brought the end with the nail down hard on the goose. It squawked and thrashed, wings flapping wildly and neck extended, trying to flee. Qin Wen stabbed the knife into its throat. It let out a brief cry and convulsed, spraying blood everywhere. Running like mad, it tried to reach the garden, but Qin Wen slammed the board against the plant pot, trapping it. Gripping the knife firmly, she thrust it again at the goose's neck. More blood spatter, a string of piercing screeches, webbed feet scrabbling at the carpet. Another attempt at escape, but its strength was ebbing. She slashed its throat twice more.

Qin Wen sat on the ground panting heavily, eyes fixed on the dead goose. As her breath steadied, she scrambled to her feet and picked up the goose by its neck. Flipping it over, she sliced open its belly and stuck both hands into its bloody insides, staining its white feathers scarlet as she rummaged around. She found an egg yolk, nothing more.

Her arms drooped, blood dripping from her dangling hands.

Yu Ling looked at the goose's corpse, unable to speak.

30

A few minutes later, the doorbell rang. They looked at each other. Qin Wen swabbed at the blood on her cheeks with her forearm, and said calmly, "You get it."

Two men stood on the doorstep, both average height, dressed similarly in thick navy blue jackets, white shirts, black belts with unobtrusive silver buckles. The only difference was one held an umbrella. The one without the umbrella asked if Qin Wen was in. There was nothing accusatory in his voice, as if this were an ordinary social call. Yu Ling said yes, and they explained that they were here to ask Qin Wen to assist with an investigation. They walked in very naturally, as if there'd never been a door there. The one with the umbrella didn't stop to put it down, perhaps so as not to add a step to their protocol, although they didn't seem to be in a hurry. The blood-soaked carpet seemed to startle them, and they shifted slightly into defensive stances.

"We killed a goose. That's not against the law, is it?" Qin

Wen came out from the bathroom. She'd cleaned her face and arms, but there were still red streaks on her clothes.

The men studied the carcass on the ground, and still seemed confused, but appeared to accept Qin Wen's explanation.

"You want me to help with an investigation, but I'm not a suspect, right? May I speak to our nanny first?"

They agreed.

"Please, have a seat. Would you like a cigarette?" She picked up the packet on the table and waved it at them, then took one herself, sliding it between her fingers and gesturing at the back garden. "We won't go far, just beneath the eaves. It's still raining, isn't it?"

They went out and found that the rain had stopped, and the sky was clearing. The thin sliver of moon was visible once more. A magpie landed on the magnolia tree, now free of blossoms, its feet gripping the branch and its tail lowered almost perpendicular to the ground, as if it were trying to mimic human posture. Yu Ling stood very straight, as if to set it an example. Her arms hung by her sides, hands curled into fists.

"You seem tense. No need for that, they're only after me. Nothing will happen to you. Would you like one? I know you smoke occasionally." She handed the cigarette packet to Yu Ling. "I might understand you better than you think."

"People like me have no secrets from you."

"You're wrong. No matter how much I learn about you, you're still a mystery to me. When I see you giving all your attention to drying our laundry, tidying up the child's toys, baking pastries, I find myself wondering what's going through your mind."

"The only thing on my mind is when I'll be able to sit down again." Yu Ling leaned over and lit her cigarette from Qin Wen's lighter.

"I'll leave Kuan Kuan with you. I know you'll take good care of him. I might not be gone long. You heard them, I'll only be helping with the investigation, right?"

"Yes, just helping with the investigation."

"I have to be honest with you: I don't know whether, when the time comes, I'll still have the money to pay your wages. I'll see what I have left. Maybe I'll sell some paintings."

"Not the Alice Neel."

"No, not that. I'll give that one to you." Qin Wen lowered her voice. "Do you think this *leverage*—could it be with his ex-wife? What if, at the crucial moment, he trusted her more?"

Yu Ling drew deeply from her cigarette, and said gravely, "I don't know."

They kept smoking. The moon faded away again. There were no clouds above them, nothing at all, just emptiness, the pale gray of a stretched canvas waiting for something to appear on it.

In the silence, Qin Wen abruptly laughed. "Us women. We always seem to be fighting over unimportant things. The things that truly matter have nothing to do with us." She flung her cigarette butt to the ground and extended her hand. "Can we be friends?"

Yu Ling lowered her eyes, finishing her cigarette. Her arm remained by her side, not making a move till Qin Wen's hand retreated and she smiled forlornly. "In any case, please take care of Kuan Kuan for me."

They went back in and found the two men waiting by the

front door. A black sedan was parked outside. The white-shirted driver raised his half-lowered window when he saw them. The men walked behind Qin Wen, escorting her to the car. The one with the umbrella took the passenger seat, the other one got in the back. The engine started and the car pulled smoothly away, speeding up and disappearing at the end of their street.

Yu Ling went back inside and shut the front door. She hurried through the dining room, up the stairs, and to her little bedroom, where she locked the door behind her and sat on the bed, taking deep breaths and staring out the window. She raised her right hand, opened the tightly clenched fist, and looked down at the black thumb drive in her palm. Silver panels extending from a black rectangle, like an insect with a metallic head. Her hand had found it on the iris-patterned carpet and she'd palmed it. As the umbrella man walked past her, she'd felt it throb, as if it might leap out and land on the floor. She'd clenched her fist tighter, digging her nails into the flesh.

Things never turned out well when she stubbornly clung to a decision she'd made, but she kept doing it. In order to protect Qin Wen, she'd made the choice to bring her disappointment rather than danger. It might break her heart, but at least it wouldn't kill her. If Qin Wen really had threatened some big shot with this leverage, she'd be putting herself on the line. Even if this person agreed for the time being, Qin Wen would be under his thumb after that. Then one day, she would suddenly vanish. So many women disappear, even famous TV presenters and athletes. They stand up to say something, then they're gone. Yu Ling believed women would never be allowed to touch most significant matters, but they lived in a perpetual fantasy, imagining themselves center stage, playing a lead role. Who said that? Like a goose believing everything it sees is smaller than itself. This goose's defective vision hadn't led to its death. It was blameless, but Yu Ling had sacrificed it. She could have stopped Qin Wen, but she'd wanted Qin Wen to utterly lose hope. Maybe she'd also felt that at this moment, it was right to sacrifice something, and what could be more fitting than the goose? It might have been full of personality, but it was just a goose. Less of a sacrifice than she'd imagined. She'd made so many bargains with fate, and this time she finally felt she wasn't on the losing end. Her only regret was not being able to shake hands with Qin Wen. They might never be friends now, but that didn't matter. She had already saved Qin Wen.

Outside, she noticed the magnolia tree had thickened its leaves, one lush clump after another filling every space, as if it had already forgotten the flowers it had shed. The blossoming felt like something from a very long time ago. She buried the goose by the magnolia tree. The ground was still soft from the rain, and it didn't take much effort. She prized up several paving stones, creating a small garden plot. When the vegetable seeds arrived, she would plant them here. Perhaps they would sprout before summer.

When the boy woke up, she told him the swan had flown away. Yes, it could fly, which proved it really was a swan. The boy seemed to understand that he ought to curb his sorrow, because swans are born to fly, and those magnificent wings had to be put to use.

"Did you see it take off?" he asked. Yu Ling knew it would be best to say no or she'd be besieged with more questions for a long time afterward, but she answered yes, she saw the whole thing, and then described to the boy how the swan had taken to the air.

Dalei called that afternoon to say he had the seeds and would bring them round after his evening shift. Yu Ling arranged to meet him at the front gate. Would she invite him inside to rest his feet and have a drink? She hadn't decided, but she was already visualizing Dalei perched at the kitchen island. She realized she very much wanted to tell him everything that had happened the previous evening.

"I changed the course of someone's life," she would say. "And there's a child involved too."

As for the thumb drive, there'd been a moment when she wanted to hand it over, to make the big shot's crimes public. But who would she give it to? Anyone she could think of might be one of the official's cronies. There was Miss Amy, of course, that lover of righteousness and defender of world peace, but Amy was so immature she'd be all too keen to sacrifice herself. Besides, deep down, Yu Ling didn't think getting rid of the big shot would change anything. You could get rid of ten people like that, and the world would still be exactly the same. The village headman would still find ways to make sure his son got the best of everything. Even if she never did anything with it, just holding the thumb drive made her feel she had power in her hands.

She decided to watch it, to see what it actually contained. That night, after Kuan Kuan had gone to bed, she went into her sir's home office and turned on the desktop. It took her quite a while to find the right slot for the drive. A new icon appeared on the scene, and she clicked on it. It only held one folder, which she opened, and there she found a file with a name consisting of random numbers and letters. The moment she opened it, she knew she'd gotten it wrong. There was no hint of danger at all. This couldn't be Qin Wen's "leverage." She'd been right: there hadn't been anything hidden behind the painting. Could it be somewhere else? Another living room, another picture? Or had this just been a drunken promise that meant nothing, a comforting and delusional hope? Music summoned her attention back to the monitor.

On the screen was this very house. The camera went in the front door and through the dining room, sweeping over the Alice Neel painting and pausing for a moment at the rosewood credenza. The back door was open and children were scampering in and out of frame, then the gazebo and rock formation appeared, and before them a greenish pond in which koi fish darted to and fro. Guests trickled out into the garden where seats had been neatly arranged. Kun opera performers, a man and a woman, went up onstage and took their positions. A cork popped and champagne frothed from a bottle. A cold buffet was laid out on the long table: vegetarian chicken, smoked fish, pork jelly, goose liver pâté. Then Yu Ling saw herself, walking past the camera with a tray of madeleines, the tip of her nose red, her gaze sluggish, eyes fixed on some distant point, just like in Qin Wen's painting. The camera abandoned her and moved among the seats, where the guests were chatting among themselves, standing to get more food even as they enjoyed the performance. The sky was darkening, and the garden lights came on, casting crisscross bamboo shadows on the white walls. The camera completed its round of the yard and stealthily crept away from the crowd, down a narrow path, to the art studio. The lights were on, but no one was there. Then the curtains slowly parted, and a red-haired clown jumped through the gap in the green velvet. He bowed deeply and batted his eyes, which were painted like gold stars. He opened his mouth in a grin that reached his ears, and waved fervently at the camera.

"Bye-bye, kiddos, bye-bye! See you again next year."

ACKNOWLEDGMENTS

I'm very grateful to my friend, the writer Lu Nei, as well as my Chinese editor, Huang Pingli, for their feedback on early drafts. Many thanks to my translator, Jeremy Tiang, who has been generous with his time as we discussed many aspects of this novel together; we have been friends for many years, and the understanding between us continues to deepen. Thanks also to my editor, Han Zhang, whose outstanding notes and edits vastly improved the manuscript, allowing it to reach its present form. I've enjoyed the process of working with her, which has given me a lot of encouragement to finish my next book.

I'm also grateful for the sacrifices that my parents have made for me, and for the support of my son. Finally, I want to thank my husband, who has given me many valuable insights on this book. More importantly, with him around, writing has become even more meaningful to me.